PRAISE FOR *SERGE*

"Reza's fourth novel is undoubtedly her most personal text, the one in which, without departing from her sense of detail and the killer line that forms her signature, she delivers herself with the most sincerity."   *VOGUE*

"Finally, a book that dares! The lightness of the irreverent Yasmina Reza is the continuation of wisdom by other means."   *THE POINT*

"What is this talent? Yasmina Reza has a gift for bringing characters to life and spicing up situations."   *MARIE CLAIRE*

"Yasmina Reza's writing is like mercury. Her story unfolds with unparalleled fluidity without us perceiving the seams."   *ELLE*

"Reza injects poetry into satire. Her art is knowing how to pierce the soul."   *LE JOURNAL DU DIMANCHE*

"A perilous tightrope act that brings beauty to our chaotic existences."   *LE PARISIEN WEEK-END*

"Reza's tragicomic pen works wonders, transforming the worst horrors into anthology scenes and our daily worries into comedies."
L'EXPRESS

"A pure delight."   *SUD OUEST*

"Reza leaves us breathless with this finely crafted little gem."
VERSION FEMININA

"In this novel with its chiseled dialogue, we love each other as much as we tear each other apart."   *LE VIF L'EXPRESS*

"Reza multiplies the comic dialogues, the incisive sallies, and these eternal scenes, which we have all experienced, which grip, beyond the imaginable." — *LE PÈLERIN*

"In this novel about siblings, old age, Jewishness, and solitude too, Yasmina Reza displays all her artistry." — *LA PROVENCE*

"A highly anticipated novel, this text, which explores the bonds of a family as diverse as it is close-knit, is deeply human." — *S THE MAGAZINE*

"With this very edgy comedy, Yasmina Reza proves that she masters the art of the novel as well as the tricks of the theater." — *LIRE*

"A breath of fresh air." — *LE SOIR*

"A novelist and playwright delights in the ups and downs of an odiously endearing clan." — *PARIS MATCH*

"That's what we love about Yasmina Reza: her freedom. And her way of using dark humor and daring to do anything." — *LA VOIX DU NORD*

"The new Yasmina Reza, of extraordinary power and truth." — *ALSACE*

"A summary of life with the scalpel of words." — *PAGE DES LIBRAIRES*

"If the author has always led her readers, with her free and subversive pen, to question the human condition, here she goes even further..." — *TÉLÉ-LOISIRS*

"Reza tackles painful subjects with lightness." FRANCE INFO

"A sumptuous novel about a family of crazy Jews. Both funny and moving." CHALLENGES

"It's great art." EUROPE 1

"While her characters provoke, fight, and resent each other, Yasmina Reza delicately leaves traces of the mutual love and shared memories that continue to bind them all together. And it is precisely this tension that constitutes this novel's strength."
ALICE DE REVIERS, *ALBERTINE*

"Here is a book that better resembles a play than a novel: a dramatic subject rooted in history; a disturbing and offbeat treatise; endearing, ridiculous, or whimsical characters; lively dialogues. But *Serge* is also an answer to the famous and very current question: can we laugh at everything?"
RODOLPHE DE SAINT HILAIRE, *CULTURE-TOPS*

"Can we say that this is one of the funniest texts written in French about a visit to Auschwitz, or is it incongruous? Funny because it is true: it is neither a farce nor a fable . . . What does it mean to be a family? What does it mean to be Jewish? The novel raises a few existential questions in passing, with great accuracy and dazzling virtuosity." NATALIE LEVISALLES, *EN ATTENDANT NADEAU*

"Hilarious. And inappropriate. But hilarious precisely because it is inappropriate. . . . . . Reza crosses every boundary between comedy and tragedy" TERESA LUXONE, *LIMINA*

ALSO BY YASMINA REZA

PLAYS

Conversations After a Burial

The Passage of Winter

Art

The Unexpected Man

Life x 3

A Spanish Play

God of Carnage

OTHER WORKS

Hammerklavier

Desolation

Adam Haberberg

Dawn Dusk or Night: A Year with Nicolas Sarkozy

How You Talk the Game

Happy Are the Happy

Bella Figura

Babylon

Anne-Marie the Beauty

YASMINA REZA

SERGE

*Translated from the French
by Jeffrey Zuckerman*

RESTLESS BOOKS
NEW YORK · AMHERST

This is a work of fiction. Names, characters, places, and incidents herein are either the products of the author's imagination or are used fictitiously. Any resemblance to actual events or persons, living or dead, is entirely coincidental.

Copyright © 2021 Flammarion
Translation copyright © 2025 Jeffrey Zuckerman

First published as *Serge* by Éditions Flammarion, Paris, 2021.

All rights reserved.

No part of this book may be reproduced or transmitted without the prior written permission of the publisher.

Restless Books and the R colophon are registered trademarks of Restless Books, Inc.

First Restless Books paperback edition August 2025

Paperback ISBN: 9781632064011
Library of Congress Control Number: 2025936456

Sholem Aleichem quotation from "Creature" in *A Treasury of Sholom Aleichem Children's Stories*, translated by Aliza Shevrin (Jason Aronson Inc., 1997).

Charlotte Delbo quotation from *Convoy to Auschwitz*, translated by Carol Cosman (Northeastern University Press, 1997).

Isaac Bashevis Singer quotation from "The Cafeteria" in *A Friend of Kafka* (1979) and reprinted in *The Collected Stories* (Farrar, Straus & Giroux, 1983).

This book is supported in part by an award from the National Endowment for the Arts.

Cover design by Daniel Benneworth-Gray
Text design and typesetting by Tetragon, London
Cover photographs by Del, Jez Timms, and Karsten Winegeart

Printed in the United States

1 3 5 7 9 10 8 6 4 2

RESTLESS BOOKS
NEW YORK • AMHERST
www.restlessbooks.org

To my Vladichka
To Magda and Imre Kertész, dear friends

SERGE

THE BÈGUES SWIMMING POOL was built in the twenties or thirties. I haven't been to a pool since grade school. Apparently, swim caps are obligatory. I brought the one I've still got from the Ouigor spa.

Just as I head for the showers, a man says: "Sir, you can't go into the pool like that."

"Why not?"

"You've got a cloth swimsuit on."

"Yes . . . ?"

"It has to be Lycra."

"I've gone for a dip in all sorts of places with this swimsuit on, and nobody's said a thing."

"Lycra's required here."

"And how am I supposed to make that happen?"

He tells me to go see the changing-room attendant. I explain my problem to the changing-room attendant. He seems a bit odd, like those folks who work as school crossing guards. He says, "Let me see what I have here." He brings me a black and brown swimsuit. A size 56, fit for Depardieu.

I say, "That's going to be too big."

"Ah, I've got a smaller one." He shows me a green one. "Two euros, please."

"That ought to fit," I say, envisioning a thirty-year-younger version of myself.

I tell Luc to get in the water. In the changing room, I strip down, start tugging the suit up my legs, and think, Shit, has this thing ever been washed? I'll have to stash away my dick. I pull at the skin to tuck away the glans, roll it all into an escargot. Make a clit of it. Then I pull up the fabric, which is basically a sausage casing, and tug and pull at it, pinching the parts between my legs nice and tight. And then a soft, whitish ruff pops up above the swimsuit. That's me. My stomach spilling over. I'll cut out bread. And wine, at some point. I get under the shower and notice Luc splashing around with his fins. What's he doing in that filthy, fungus-ridden footbath area?! Two and a half meters that I'm tiptoeing around as gingerly as a wading bird so as not to set foot in it. I haul out the kid, who's determined to stay put. It's just a wading pool to him, but for me it might as well be the Ganges.

In the pool proper, I try to teach him how to do the breaststroke. He's nine—at his age, kids are already swimmers. I show him: prayer, then submarine, then airplane, but he doesn't care, he just wants to play. He's bouncing every which way, splashing wildly, almost drowning. I drag him out, he's like a rat with his snaggletooth. He's bent over laughing. His mouth's agape. I gesture for him to shut it whenever he's not right by me. He copies me to please me, squints his eyes, presses his lips tight, and bares that gaping maw again.

In the street, I'd explained how to cross it. I broke down the movement: BEFORE you cross, look left, then look right, and then left again. He does it all well enough, mimicking me with a slowness I can't believe. It doesn't occur to him that there's a reason for these motions; all he thinks is that wriggling his hips and twisting his neck are the key to crossing. He doesn't get that it's to see the cars. He does it to make me happy. Ditto for reading. He reads the words, sure, but he doesn't get them, not usually. I tell him: keep an eye out for the periods, when you see a period, stop and breathe. He gives it a go out loud: *The eldest took the mill, the second the donkey, and the youngest nothing but the cat.* I say, Period! He stops. He inhales deeply and exhales slowly through his mouth. When he starts again—*The poor young fellow was quite comfortless for having received so little*—nobody has the least clue now what the whole thing is about.

∽

There were mornings when I would take him to preschool; he'd go into the courtyard and start playing on his own. He'd pretend to be a train. He'd race around, making a racket, *choo-choo*, not playing with friends. I'd linger for a bit, in the background, peering through the railings. Nobody would talk to him.

I do like this kid. He's more interesting than most. I've never been entirely sure who I am to him. There was a stretch of time when he would see me in his mother's bedroom. I've stayed close with Marion so I won't lose the kid. But I don't think he realizes. Am I being completely honest about that? He calls me Jean. That's my name. When he says it, it seems even shorter.

Does his mother worry about him? Marion thinks that if she buys enough things—ski masks, handkerchiefs, antiseptics, mosquito repellent, tick repellent, you-name-it repellent—she can protect him from life. She's like my mother that way, actually. A woman who shipped Serge and me off to Jewish summer camp in Corvol with a 110-kilo bag. A complete pharmacy. There were adders that year. There were adders every year.

Marion's been in love with another man for several weeks now. So much the better. He's broke and going through a divorce. She pays for it all: restaurants, movies, presents just for him. It amazes her how willingly he accepts this state of affairs.

"He doesn't complain," she says. "Free-minded. A man to the core."

"Of course," I say.

Marion's exhausting. With her, the tiniest thing can spin out of control in a split second. One night, after a nice dinner out, I drove her back to her place and dropped her off. I wasn't even at the end of the street when my phone rang.

"I was attacked in the lobby!"

"Attacked! Wait, when?"

"Just now."

"But I dropped you off a second ago."

"You took off as soon as I shut the door."

"And you were attacked?"

"You didn't even wait for me to get to the porch, you were off and away, like you couldn't wait to be rid of me."

"Of course not."

"It's the truth!"

"I'm sorry. I wasn't paying attention. Marion, were you attacked or not?"

"But that's what I'm saying. You never pay attention. You don't care."

"No, no."

"The front door wasn't even open and you drove off without a second glance. I turned to give you a wave and all I saw was the back of your neck, ten meters off already!"

"I'm sorry. You're not going to cry, are you?"

"Oh, I am."

"Where are you now?"

"In the lobby."

"Did the assailant leave?"

"You're very funny."

"Marion . . ."

"Can't you see how humiliating this is? You turn around with a smile and a sweet little wave, and your ride's already gone, he didn't look twice, didn't check, not even the bare minimum at night, to make sure you got in safe!"

"You're right. You should go on up now . . ."

"It's just good manners!"

"That it is."

"Just plop down the package and *whoosh*!"

"Yes, yes, I should have waited."

"And given *me* a wave."

"Mm-hmm, given you a wave."

"Come on back and give me that wave."

"I'm at place du Général-Houvier."

"Come back here, I can't just go on up and get to bed like this."

"Marion, you're being childish."

"So what if I am?"

"Marion, I've just lost my mother . . ."

"Oh, there it is! I knew you'd say it. What's that got to do with anything?"

∽

Our mother's last words were "LCI." The last words of her life. After we'd placed that horrible medical bed in front of the TV, my brother said, "Maman, do you want to watch some TV?" My mother said "LCI." The bed had been delivered and she'd been put in it. She died that very night without another word.

She wouldn't discuss it. That medical bed haunted her. All and sundry had been singing its praises, purportedly because she'd be more comfortable, but actually everyone had been leaning over her usual far-too-low bed, the big double bed in which our father had died, and it was breaking their backs. She didn't get up anymore. All the bodily functions that cancer had thrown out of whack were now carried out in the bed. Someone had to convince us of the advantages of a medical bed. We'd ordered it unbeknownst to her. It had been delivered at dawn by two men who'd taken their sweet time putting it together. The room was overrun by such a bewildering arsenal of medical and electronic devices that Serge and I now had no place to stand. She didn't put up the least protest at being effused from one place to the next. They tried out several buttons. She was up high, half-dazed, helpless, suffering the ludicrous tilting up and down. They'd set the head of the bed against a sidewall on which a calendar with Putin petting a cheetah had been pinned. She couldn't see out the window anymore, her small and beloved square of garden, and she wearily stared straight ahead. In her own bedroom, she was practically adrift. The calendar was a gift from a Russian home health nurse. My mother had a weakness for Putin, she thought he had sad eyes. Once the men were gone, we decided to put her in her usual position, namely, facing the window and in front of the TV. We had to move the big bed. The mattress first, a mattress from time immemorial that proved to be unbelievably heavy, flabby, and seemingly filled with sand. Serge and I dragged it as best we could into the hallway, falling over several times. We left the base of the bed in her room, upright against a wall. We wheeled in Maman and the medical bed to face the window and the TV again. Serge said, "Do you want to see the TV?" We sat on each side of the bed in folding chairs from the kitchen. It was four days after the attack at the Vivange-sur-Sarre Christmas market; LCI was broadcasting the memorial ceremony for the victims. The only word the correspondent had on her lips was "remembrance," a word drained of meaning. The same girl said after several shots of candy stores and painted boxes, "Life may go on, but nothing will be the same."

"You're wrong," Serge said, "everything will be exactly the same. In twenty-four hours."

Not one word out of our mother ever again. Nana and her husband Ramos came in the afternoon. My sister shrieked, her head buried in her husband's shoulder, "Oh, that bed is a nightmare!" Maman died that very night, without getting to make use of the new equipment's features. So long as things stayed as they always had, she could weather this illness's innumerable vicissitudes. But the medical bed had sealed her lips. No, the medical bed, that monstrosity smack-dab in the middle of her bedroom, had sealed her fate.

∽

Once she was dead, things went off the rails.

"Mamie, you were the one holding this mishmash of a family together," my niece Margot said at the cemetery.

Our mother had been a stickler for our family lunches every Sunday. Even after she'd moved to her ground-floor place in the banlieues. Even in our Paris years, our Papa years, those Sunday lunches barely did anything for the general atmosphere of panic and hypertension. Nana and Ramos came with heaps of out-of-the-world victuals—Levallois chicken, the best chicken in the world (handpicked on the farm by the butcher), or a leg of Levallois lamb that was every bit as incomparable. The rest—French fries, green peas, ice cream—was straight from the ice chests at Picard. My brother and my sister came with their family, I always came solo. Joséphine, Serge's daughter, came to the doorstep every other week already exasperated. Victor, Nana and Ramos's son, was training at the École Émile Poillot, the "Harvard of gastronomy," according to Ramos, who pronounces it "Harward." At our table was a future *grand chef*. We had him carve the leg of lamb and applauded his great skill, and my mother apologized for the incorrect utensils and the frozen vegetables (she'd never enjoyed cooking; the advent of frozen food had changed her whole life).

We rushed to sit down and eat as if we were in a rented room with just twenty minutes until we had to clear out for a Japanese wedding. There was no making headway on any particular topic, no following any story to its end. A surreal soundscape with my brother-in-law filling in its lower frequencies. Ramos Ochoa is a man who rather relishes never hurrying and makes sure you know it. We would hear him say, belatedly, in a sepulchral and ostentatiously modulated voice, "Could you pass the wine please, thank you so much, Valentina." Valentina being Serge's latest significant other. Ramos may have been born in France, but his family is Spanish. They're all Podemos. He and my sister live in poverty, not without some pride.

At one of those lunches, just as the galette des rois came, my mother said, "Isn't anyone going to ask me how my routine checkup went?" (She'd had breast cancer nine years earlier.)

Back in the day, she would crow about snagging two crowns when the bakers were only putting one in each cake. The galette must have gone into the oven at the start of the meal. She wouldn't hear of Valentina, our Italian darling, biting into a cold galette! Nana had set the half-charred thing on the table but, thank God, the little trinket hadn't been sighted yet. Each year we would bicker over it, my mother would cheat and slip it to a kid, and the kids would bicker over it. One year when she didn't get it, Margot, Victor's little sister, flung her plate with her portion of galette out the window. Now there were only teenagers and old folks, apart from Valentina's ten-year-old son. He slipped under the table, Nana cut the slices, and little Marzio handed out the plates.

"How did your routine checkup go?"

"Oh, I've got a blotch on my liver."

∾

Sitting on the edge of the big double bed in the dark room a few months later, Serge said, "Maman, where do you want to be buried?"

"Nowhere. I don't really care."

"Do you want to be with Papa?"

"No! Not with the Jews!"

"Where do you want to be?"

"Not at Bagneux."

"Do you want to be cremated?"

"Cremated. And that's my final word on the topic."

We had her cremated and we took her to Bagneux to the Popper family plot. Where else? She didn't like the sea or the countryside. Or any place where her dust might be one with the land.

∾

At the Père-Lachaise funeral home, there were about ten of us. The three children and grandchildren. Zita Feifer, her childhood friend, as well as Madame Antoninos, the hairdresser, who'd come until Maman's last days to dye the few wisps on her scalp and pluck the thick hairs growing on her chin. There was also Carole, Serge's first wife, Joséphine's mother. Zita was fresh from surgery on both hips. A funeral home staffer dragged her toward the elevator in which we watched her with her canes, stunned, disappearing into the floor of the dead.

Once underground, she was taken into an empty room where, between two trestles, her friend's coffin waited. She had only just sat down when, without any warning, at ear-splitting volume and for no discernible reason, Brahms's "Hungarian Dance No. 5" rang out. After ten minutes of isolation and Romany music, Zita dragged herself to the door, pleading for help.

In the meantime, I'd found Serge outside smoking in front of the Audi he'd driven there.

"Whose is that?"

"It's mine."

"Yeah, right."

"It belongs to one of Chicheportiche's friends, some car dealer. You'd think it's a production car, but it's actually a race car. Cheaper than a Porsche and just as high-performing . . ."

"Huh."

"Chicheportiche brings him buyers and he loans him one of these bad boys every so often. It's a V8, it's got the horsepower of a Mustang or a Ferrari. You know, it's like you've got the best of a 911 and of a Panamera. They're gonna buy up the lot so they can build an office block."

"I thought you called it quits with Chicheportiche."

"I did, but he's buddy-buddy with the mayor of Montrouge."

"Fair enough."

"Look what I found."

He took a sheet of paper folded in four from his pocket and held it out. A letter very carefully written in more than merely familiar handwriting with thin blue ink:

My Pitounet, I hope everyone's gotten here safe and sound and not all overheated. At the bottom of the suitcase you'll find a little surprise to share with Jean. I'm counting on the two of you, and especially you, my Pitounet, not to eat the whole thing in one day! You'll also find a Famous Five book and that collection of African tales. Apparently Five Have a Wonderful Time *is a real treat. That's what the bookseller said. Don't forget to rub on some Pipiol if you have any stings before going to sleep and remind your brother, when he takes off his glasses, to put them away in their case. You know he's scatterbrained. Have fun, my Pitounet. Your loving Maman.*

"Pipiol's still a thing," I said. "Nowadays it's a spray."

"No kidding?"

He tucked the letter back into his pocket and scrolled through pictures on his phone. He stopped on a photo of Maman posing like a queen not even a year ago with her paper crown.

"The last galette," he intoned.

"Come on," I replied, "they're waiting for us."

∼

In the funeral home's snug little underground room, Margot, looking serious the way only some children can, read a text of her own. "Mamie, you didn't exercise a day in your life, but you got a stationary bike because the oncologist prescribed light physical activity. You agreed to pedal a bit in your nightgown and your fleece jacket so long as the resistance level was 1 out of 8. You got in position like those Tour de France cyclists you saw on TV, you hunched over the handlebars while your feet felt around for the pedals hanging there. One time, when you were cycling super slow and staring at your dear Vladimir Putin, I shifted the resistance up to 2. Good job, Mamie! I'm so happy to see you do this! You said you're the only one . . . You never wanted to have muscles or that sort of thing and you didn't see any point in the final stages. I don't know if where you are now—where are you?—you'll think it's wise for me to talk about the stationary bike. I'm telling this story to make people laugh but really to remember how courageous and obedient you were. And fatalist. You accepted your fate. Your sons spent their time scolding you, even when you were sick, telling you off for your habits, your black humor, your taste, your forgetfulness, the presents you gave us, the candy, you'd let them lecture you and you'd act sheepish, but you were the one holding it all together, Mamie, our whole mishmash of a family was being held together by you. In your little backyard in Asnières, you were growing an Austrian pine. A fifteen-centimeter stub because that was cheaper. 'Maman thinks she'll live forever,' Uncle Jean used to say, 'she's sure that when she turns three hundred sixty-two, she'll walk around the tree with Margot's great-granddaughter.' I don't know what your children will do with your apartment, Mamie, but I'm going to transplant your pine someplace where you'll always be able to walk around it with us, even if nobody knows it."

Who got it in their head to have this Hungarian dance music on? Margot had just turned around to sit down beside her mother in tears and was hugging her tight when a frenzied violin began whipping up our little group. Who picked this out? Our mother did like Brahms, yes, but the romantic Brahms of the Lieder. Behind me, Zita Feifer shrieked, "Not again!" And then the coffin was brought around the bier on a rolling cart, and Marta Popper went through a small door on the left and was gone.

∽

Upon leaving Père-Lachaise, we put Zita in a cab and went to sit on the terrace at a nearby café. Joséphine went straight to the bathroom. It was nice out the way it sometimes can be in December. When she returned, she stopped in her tracks and, still standing, made a face because there were no more seats in the sun. Joséphine's a makeup artist and always overdoes her own face. When she pouts, her mouth turns into a bitter chili pepper.

Nana wanted to get up and offer her seat, but Carole stopped her.

"It's no trouble," Nana said.

"But you shouldn't have to be the one in the shade!"

The hairdresser said, "Take my seat, Joséphine, I'm not one for the sun."

"You stay put where you are, Madame Antoninos!" Carole ordered.

"But I haven't asked for anything! Don't you have anything better to do than fixate on me?"

"You're getting on our nerves, Joséphine."

"It's freezing, why are we sitting outside? I don't get why Mamie wanted to be cremated. It's insane for a Jew to choose cremation."

"That was her wish."

"After everything her family's been through . . . cremation!"

"Oh, will you quit being a pain in the ass," Victor said.

She was still standing, twisting some locks in her curly mop of hair.

"I've decided that I'm going to Osvitz this year."

"Unfortunately it's closed."

"AOSHWITZ!" Serge shrieked. "'Osvitz'!! Like the goys! Learn how to say it right! Auschwitz! Auschhhhhwitz! *Shhhh*!"

"Ugh, Papa!"

"Everyone can hear you," Nana whispered.

"I won't have my daughter saying Osvitz! Where'd she pick that up?"

"Don't look at me!" Carole said.

"Here we go again, making it all about her!"

"Jo, be better than him," Nana muttered as Joséphine made her way toward the sidewalk.

"A travesty of an education! Wait, where'd she go? Joséphine, where are you going now?! You know, I paid through the nose for a course in eyebrows, and look where that's gotten her, now she wants to go to Auschwitz, what's wrong with this girl?"

Once Joséphine was out of sight behind a building on Place Magenta, Carole got up to run after her.

"Would it kill you to let her be for just once in your life?"

"Look at her! She's always going on and on."

Ramos said, with that sepulchral voice of his, "Hell of a smog machine, yeah?"

"What are you talking about?"

"The Audi."

"Oh! A smog machine, yeah."

∾

This morning, crossing rue Pierre-Lerasé, I noticed a small green Paris municipal vehicle, one of those tiny things for washing and sweeping sidewalks. And who should be in the driver's seat but my brother-in-law! I walked over. In that brief, inquisitorial movement, a thought lit up my head: It's not enough for Ramos Ochoa to be sneaky and land himself unemployment benefits with all the short-term jobs he lines up just so, along with his hush-hush IT work, but he's also snagged a sweet little Sunday job that doesn't require anything more than a driver's license. In the infinite free time he's somehow got no matter his obligations, he's found himself another new under-the-table revenue stream to plump up his retirement! All the while Ramos's been driving the vehicle with a casual fastidiousness, and his complacency in the driver's seat is reminiscent of his typical overbearingness at home. As I get closer, of course it turns out not to be Ramos Ochoa. But the image was so convincing that it put the finishing touch on my perception of the guy.

Ramos Ochoa might not be one of the A-list names in this story, but I do like talking about him. And who's to say that he, like so many supporting characters, won't become a prominent one, given my shameful propensity for criticizing him?

He came off nice and worthy enough at first. An IT network tech working for Unilever (before getting himself fired), the son of a housemaid and a construction worker—what could we hold against him? Our father, who never bothered with any progressive talk, made it clear he was against this union. That Anne Popper, his pearl, should wed a Spaniard from God knows what village in Cantabria was a detestable thought. He saw his daughter as a "princess"—he said the word with evident scorn and pride alike—and he couldn't understand how someone like Ramos Ochoa, who in another era might have bitten right into a raw onion, barefoot under a blazing sun, could be worthy of her. Of course, we were all wrong about him. The "in" thing was happiness, not old patriarchal values. At that point, happiness wasn't just in shouting distance of desire but the be-all and end-all of pretty much any philosophy. That might have been what did my father in. A year after Ramos Ochoa turned up, shyly holding Nana's hand in the rue Pagnol entryway, my father was dispatched by colon cancer.

These days I find myself thinking that, with all the underhanded tortures and torments we inflicted, Serge and I very well might have driven Nana into the warm embrace of someone like Ramos Ochoa. Childhood doings are permanently carved God knows where. When I hear about some fresh horror on the radio and that the victims are in their sixties, I think, Whew! That's a shame for them, but at least they've had themselves a full life already. And then I think, They're your age, pal, and practically Serge's or Nana's! How did you not clock that? At my mother's place, on her bedside table, there was a picture of the three of us tangled up in a wheelbarrow, laughing. It's like we've all been shoved in and tossed into real time.

I don't know how we siblings ended up staying as thick as thieves: we aren't that similar or that close to one another. Siblings tend to disperse, go their own ways, bound only by a thin thread of sentimentality or conventionality. Anyone can see that Serge and Nana have long belonged to that grown-up demographic of humanity that I'm supposed to belong to as well, but that's mere appearance. Deep down, I'm still the middle child, Nana is still our parents' little girl, their pretentious favorite but also the second-in-command in our war games, the slave, the Japanese prisoner, the traitor who gets stabbed—in our room, she was never a girl but a corporal or a martyr—and my brother is still the eldest son, leading his men with a dangling chinstrap and death's conspiratorial smile, he's the daredevil, the Dana Andrews, and I'm the follower, the blank slate: if the eldest son jumps off a bridge, then so do I. We didn't have a TV at home, but Cousin Maurice did. We called him Cousin Maurice, but in fact he was a distant relative of my father's on some Russian side. The only member of our family apart from our parents who we'd really known. Serge and I would go to his place on rue Raffet every Sunday and binge on American movies. We'd lie down in front of the screen with a Coke and a straw and we'd watch *Merrill's Marauders* or *The Dam Busters*, which I really liked, or some good old Western. For ages, I thought of Indians as folks hell-bent on being evil and scalping women. It wasn't until I saw Alan Ladd and Richard Widmark that I started to respect redskins. Later on, Cousin Maurice took us to the Champs-Élysées. He had a camel-hair coat, an astrakhan hat, and a body built like a brick shithouse. Our best memory was seeing Richard Fleischer in Le Normandie starring in *The Vikings*, a terrifying film with Kirk Douglas (Maurice pointed and shrieked "Russian Jew!" whenever Kirk appeared) and a young Tony Curtis. Nowadays kids under twelve wouldn't be allowed to see it. Back then, we hadn't yet had our fill of images; we came out of a movie like explorers of a vast new realm. That was the texture of our brotherhood. A jungle with curtains, landings, parachute flights, sacrifices, and Nana bound and gagged, Burmese hell, it was, before erotic temptations dared to trouble our purity, the stuff of our hours of glory and suffering: a jumble in a wheelbarrow.

∼

Luc asks questions about God. He doesn't say "God," he says "the God." "Why doesn't the God want us to tell lies?" (I tried to answer and got all muddled up.) We look at maps together. He's mad about maps: relief maps, road maps, even Ordnance Survey maps. He likes rivers; I explain how water moves. I explain that the Souloise flows into the Drac, which in turn flows into the Isère.

"And what does the Isère flow into?"
"The Rhône."
"And the Rhône?"
"Into the sea."

I don't know how he visualizes all these waterways flowing. He knows that I study those cables that carry electricity. He wants to know where I find electricity. I sketch the big picture with fire, wind, and water. I show him how primary energy is transformed into secondary energy; I draw turbines, the rotor, the stator, and the way all that creates a magnetic field, which produces an electric current. For hours he repeats "rotor, stator, rotor, stator, rotor, stator," bobbing his head and windmilling his arms.

One day we happened upon a plaque in front of a drain: *The sea begins here*. I said, "Yes, that's to keep folks from tossing in their cigarette butts and other junk."

"But does the sea really begin here?"

"Well, yeah."

I buy him some Brio and Kapla sets. He makes cities with intersections, bridges, storage tanks, forests, lighthouses. He includes pylons with intertwined wires that stretch down and disappear underground because I described electricity in the city as a spiderweb. As he arranges things, he makes noises and chimes. He has a corner to himself at my place and I'd never destroy what he's made. Every so often, when he's not there, I scrutinize the model and think, Oh, huh, it'd be a good idea to put a fence here. I take one or two Kaplas lying around and make a fence. He comes back, sometimes a month later, furrows his brow, and immediately takes out what I've put in. I've decided that I should introduce him to Marzio, Valentina's son. The timing could be better, considering that Valentina actually fired Serge from her place and isn't talking to him anymore. I have to be careful not to put a foot wrong.

Luc likes any game where we're facing each other. Like chess. But the rules don't interest him. He's perfectly happy to pull out the checkerboard, sit down facing me, ensconced in his chair, and set up the pieces. I explained how each piece moves, and he likes to play at playing. He can't do that with someone his age like Marzio. Marzio's competitive. He wants to compare himself and come out bigger. Being friends with that kind of boy would help Luc, I think. I've seen him get sad in parks. He'd go up to children but they wouldn't look at him, like he was invisible. He's too shy. In first grade he had a teacher he hugged. For no reason. She told Marion and was so moved she started crying. She said, "He has some speech problems and his head's in the clouds." She only ever explained his problems or his backwardness as "his head's in the clouds."

༶

It used to be that when you didn't know what someone did, you said "import-export"; nowadays, you say "consulting." If someone asks Serge what he does, he'll say "consultant." Serge was always the king of murky business. When I was studying at Supélec, he was set on being the leader in spreadable products alongside a Ferrero veteran whom he'd talked into hanging out his shingle. The poor guy poured his whole severance package into it. All the while, Serge was courting café and pub owners.

He took a cut of exclusivity agreements. That was his first somewhat lucrative work, more or less on schedule.

When we were little, we shared a bedroom. At fourteen, he was already a man—well, he took himself for a man. His voice had settled into a bass, he had a beard and marked sexual appeal. Add to that a brother two years younger, me, who ate up practically all his chest-thumping. Serge bragged about being a lady-killer. In fact, he was small, clumsy, and acne-ridden. It was ages before anyone took a liking to him. Girls snickered behind his back. I saw them with my own eyes in the school hallways. After all the battles and heroic dreams, Serge had his sights on a future in music. He got into guitar and sang in a language nobody could make sense of. He tried out all sorts of looks. We didn't say "look" back then, I don't know what we said. None of them suited him. I remember his Bowie look in particular, such an absurd look given the difference in proportions.

"You've got makeup on!" my father said in bewilderment.

"All the rock stars have makeup on."

"Not Jean Ferrat!"

His hair was an issue. Frizzy and scant, barely affected by the treatments of the time. After a few attempts at a Hendrix-esque afro, Serge opted to grow it out. His hair formed two wings atop his scalp that spread out to form a frothy teepee on his shoulders. Every so often he used rollers to make it wavy. He used plenty of hairspray, laughing it off, putting on a bit of a swagger, but I could tell he wasn't totally self-assured. At some point, a girl, not an amazing one, came to listen to records at the house. Serge considered himself an expert on British rock; the floor of our bedroom was heaped up with sleeves for the Clash, the Who, Dr. Feelgood, and so on . . . Serge acted as a huckster for a record seller across the boulevard, and in exchange the guy offered him the latest goods. At some point, he went there with his friend Jacky Alcan wearing his father's hunting jacket. The jacket had a huge back pocket open on both sides that Serge discreetly slipped LPs into. I was often dragged along to keep a lookout.

One day our father walked into the room. He sat on one of the beds, bent over in silence, with his hands together between his legs. Then he said, "Where did they come from? All these goods, where did they come from?"

"The record dealer and I have a handshake agreement. I send half the school his way."

"Where's this dealer?"

"Rue Bredaine. Two stations down."

"He's awfully generous, I'll say. You think you'll open up a shop of your own?"

"Ha ha ha."

"Jean, how come you're not laughing?"

"But I am, I'm laughing, didn't you hear me?"

He grabbed the sleeve of *Deep Purple in Rock* and stared blankly at the band members carved into Mount Rushmore with their hair like Louis XIV wigs.

"And that smoke I smell in the bathroom, neither of you know whose fault that is, I imagine?"

"No, Papa."

The slap came right away. The sort of big loud slap he knew how to give, and, I should add, to Serge alone, never to Nana or me.

Our father, Edgar Popper, a small bald man at home in petrol-blue suits, used to smoke Gauloises and Mehari's Ecuador for years until a bout of pneumonia forced him to quit. He made no allowances for his old weaknesses, let alone for having sworn off of them. He was who he now was, his forgetful brain allowing him to change his principles and mindsets again and again. Serge was accustomed to such fits of rage. He put up no fight, but his eyes reddened and I could see him holding back tears. I could see his cheek swelling and reddening. If I tried to offer him any comfort, he'd push me away.

"If he thinks I'd actually condescend to smoke, he's a moron!"

And the father, in turn, struggled to get over his own bouts. When he landed too hard or too clumsy of a slap, he'd often have to go lie down in the throes of low-level heart trouble. Our mother would jump up to give Serge a talking-to: "See the state you've put your papa in! Go and make nice with him." From time to time, he did. Less so over the years.

It was unfair. Our mother knew it, but she opted for cold indifference. She was an elusive mother, capable of tender and harsh words alike, of stifling overprotectiveness and neglect. She played with dolls when it came to Nana, dressed her up in stiff clothes that were not to be gotten dirty or wrinkled, covered her hurriedly in kisses, and tried to get rid of her quickly whenever the child started whining. I felt like we were a hindrance, but to what exactly was never clear.

The father received Serge lying down and anxious. The mother stood in the hallway and monitored the ceasefire. Serge quietly stood straight, looking for a spot on the quilted bedspread on which to fix his gaze. They stayed like that until the father raised a magnanimous hand that Serge took weakly. And then the father pulled him in close and they hugged each other. No words exchanged. Both men came out of their nastiness followed by embraces feeling rather bitter. It took some time for things to be cheery again.

I should add that my father's suspicions regarding a storefront weren't too far-fetched. Some years later, on Passage Brady, with that very same Jacky Alcan and his hunting jacket, Serge opened a record shop where they sold books, fanzines, discs, posters, and concert gewgaws. Le Metal is still going strong, bigger than ever, and now under management on Boulevard Magenta.

My father was a Motul salesman. In the early seventies, Motul brought out the 300V Century, a one-hundred-percent synthetic lubricant for motor racing. Talking about his company and himself, the word "pioneer" came to his lips quickly. He was invited to Le Mans every year. In 1972, he smiled as he shook the hand of Pompidou, "that anti-Semitic bastard," he'd called him until that handshake, "who had pardoned that despicable man Touvier and secretly sold smoke and mirrors to Gaddafi while he was hanging Israel out to dry!" The framed photo of that encounter on the racetrack was propped for all to see on the decorative chimney lintel in the living room. Pompidou and he were the same height and evidently had some shared physical kinship. The word "anti-Semitic" was replaced by "pragmatic." "He's a pragmatic man," my father would sigh as he added, "he doesn't see the point of bickering with Arabs, they've got the oil so what's a man to do!"

The wallops would be over just like that. The real thing about fatherly violence was how disproportionate and unexpected it was. When Serge got into his teens, he too started having bouts of anger as unforeseeable as the blows he withstood. He was so thin-skinned, so high-strung. Just a minor comment could set him off. And questions of the most general sort, political or otherwise, could make him lose his temper even though there was no clear logic to his beliefs. He'd leave the table in a huff and the room in a rage, all but destroying the door. We had two madmen in the house.

My father was always irritated. When someone commented on his hotheadedness, which Maman and Nana ventured once heads were cooled—a cool head, imagine that!—he would say, "I'm not hotheaded, I have responsibilities, nobody here knows what that means, nobody has any idea what kind of burden I'm shouldering, for my dear ladies' sake, for this family's well-being! And what do I get out of it? Whining and whining. Oh, I'm hotheaded? Well, thank you. Sure, I'm hotheaded, since you've got me all worked up. Why do you think my hair's falling out? Why my skin's getting all scaly and patchy? Why do you think?"

Regarding his skin, at some point a doctor said, "Yes, you've got psoriasis. You must have had a close brush with death recently."

∽

My father didn't care about me. I was the boring old good boy who made no trouble, "did exactly like his brother" and "had no personality." Unlike Serge, who drove him crazy with his brainless opinions, his looks, his dirty tricks, and who he in turn drove crazy with his violence and his theoretically enlightening arguments that, practically, just caught him off guard and maybe even made an impression. It was appreciably quieter at home when Serge wasn't there—around fifteen or sixteen Serge got into his dealings (racketeering, trafficking, we didn't know the half of it) and was around less and less—but we weren't made for calm. A vague boredom lingered, we bickered over little things, the days became monotonous and lifeless. In a Russian book I recently read this line: "After military service I came to understand just how lifeless civil life was."

The only thing that was certain to liven up our days was a conversation about Israel. With Israel, we fell right into grandiloquence and pathos. Our relatives had passed away and left behind nothing but fragments, remnants of potentially cooked-up biographies, and there weren't words for how riveting we found their sagas. Who wants to be burdened with religion and the dead? We don't talk enough about the lightness of no heritage. But we had Israel! That was the word Father had for filling the immense historical silence and remaining steadfast. Our forebears had fought with God on this earth: we weren't poor souls adrift with nothing to rally around. We had Israel. With Israel, the Poppers had something to feed their madness. The word alone was enough to set off a nice little bout whether or not Serge was around to add his two cents. Our mother had no sympathy for Israel. Marta Heltaï (her father was born Frankel, but the preceding generation had Magyarized the last name) came from a family that had done well in the wool industry. Her parents, apostles of assimilation, had stamped out every whiff of Jewishness. She and her brother had gone to high school at a Lutheran institution. All four of them had left Hungary after the war to escape the Soviets, had mysteriously escaped deportation even as close relatives (brothers and parents) were as good as dead in the '44 spring convoys. A version still maintained in thinly veiled terms by Zita Feifer and confirmed by the archives. But my mother made no mention of it in her lifetime. The fundamental fact of not belonging to the Jewish world had extended to the world of the persecuted. She had this outdated propensity to be wholly disconnected from the world of "victims." Nor did she have any fondness for this State that, in her opinion, was ultimately baring an indelible scar to the world. My father wasn't of the same mind at all. The Poppers were middle-class Viennese Jews with half a foot in the avant-garde and another (also half) in the synagogue. Grandfather, a mechanical engineer, managed to get his wife and son out of the country after the Anschluß. He himself, as well as his mother and sister, died in Theresienstadt. In my father's eyes, Israel, blessed be its name, was the place of reparations and of Jewish genius. Israel was a place to hope for anything, even the miraculous. How many times had David and Goliath been invoked, a small country up against two hundred million Arabs: "They ran so fast they left behind their shoes," he laughed after the Six-Day War. How often had the Garden of Eden been boasted of, an orchard in bloom where there had been just Bedouins and camel dung. When we ate oranges at home, he was in the habit of asking if they were from Jaffa.

Anyone who didn't revere Israel—the only, only democracy in the region!—was anti-Semitic. Full stop. He would add, "Don't listen to your mother, she's anti-Semitic."

"But she's Jewish," we might dare to say.

"Those are the worst! The worst anti-Semites are Jews! Get that in your head."

And to drive the point home, and denigrate her family in the bargain, he added, "Don't you forget that there's nothing more shameful than a shameful Jew!"

"What do folks need Israel for?" Maman would say. "Look at all the problems that's stirred up."

"The Jews need Israel."

"Do we need to be Jewish? We're not religious."

"She doesn't get it."

"The kids don't feel Jewish. Do you kids feel Jewish?"

"And whose fault is that? Twist the knife in the wound, why don't you! Whose fault is it if the kids don't feel Jewish? Mine? Oh yes, it's my fault because I listened to you! They didn't get any Sunday school, they don't know a thing, my sons haven't even had their bar mitzvah! I resent that. I really do resent that I didn't put my foot down."

"They went to Jewish summer camp."

"Commies!"

"How are they going to learn, Edgar, if they don't have any example to follow?"

"And who's setting the example? Who's the bedrock of the house with any Jewish family, Marta? The wife! It's the wife who lights the candles!"

"Candles!"

As soon as the candles came up, my mother would burst out laughing.

He spat, through bitterly clenched teeth, that she didn't understand a thing, this lady didn't understand a thing.

As soon as Serge started laughing too, he would get a walloping straightaway.

"She's not much of a thinker," the father would say. "Pretty flighty."

Did his own mother light the candles? Who knew. She got remarried to a shoe salesman from Nice. We barely knew her.

By contrast, communism—their common bête noire—united them. When it came to communism, my father had totally different opinions, and my mother adored his wisecracks.

One time we saw Andrei Gromyko on the news and my father said, "Look at how that man laughs. That's what they teach you in Moscow. Laugh! Laugh! And you know, Marta, that's not an easy laugh to make, that's a Marxist laugh! Ha ha ha."

In hopes of making us feel closer to his beloved Israel, one summer my father sent Serge and me there under the watchful eye of Cousin Maurice, who had studied in Jerusalem in the late thirties. The oft-mentioned concept of a kibbutz had always drawn a blank. Serge was seventeen, I was fourteen. For Maurice, Israel meant the Sheraton and the beach in Tel Aviv. He had no interest in schlepping two little brats around on an educational tour. So he arranged for a full week of some tour operator taking us to various corners of the country. The day after we landed, we got up at dawn for the bus to Jerusalem. Average age: one hundred. As we reached the heights of the city, which we could still see—a dizzying sight—stretching out below us, before exurban ugliness prevailed, before the hills were wholly covered in concrete, before the city, like so many others, was no longer visibly positioned in a landscape, we were treated to "Yerushalayim Shel Zahav" being blasted from the crackling speakers up front and belted out by part of the group too. We got out and made our way single file down the alleyways, led by a sweat-drenched woman shaking a yellow flag. Serge said, "This is worse than death." He dragged me by the arm to a street corner and we headed in a different direction.

That very night, we informed Maurice of our decision to leave the group and the organized tour.

He immediately flew into a rage, shouting in the hotel lobby, "You little shits will do no such thing, I paid for the whole thing upfront!"

"They can reimburse us," Serge said.

"Absolutely not! You idiot. Jews never reimburse!"

Of the remainder of that first stay, I remember a red car and a peculiar Dov who took us to Acre, I remember dropping my plate of earthy-tasting hummus in a goldfish tank behind his back, and that's pretty much it.

༄

Cousin Maurice has attained the age of ninety-nine. And now he's bedridden, a prisoner on rue Raffet. It's the darkest apartment on earth, a darkness made darker by the weight of the heavy curtains and the plaster replicas and the old paintings. At Maurice's, nothing's moved in years. As if bladder cancer weren't enough, he broke all his bones a few months ago tumbling down the stairs of a Russian restaurant. So he's in a medical bed too, with a bag on the side holding the contents from a catheter. His bed's lower and cozier than our mother's, though. In other words, the equipment blends in with the room. Whenever I come to see him, clucking, fleeting shadows leave the room—the women in his life, legal wives (three in all, although the first one, the American one, went back to the motherland), mistresses, secretaries, or podiatrists who take turns distracting their darling. The women are brave. "No,"

Maurice says, "the women are nurses at heart, they like tucking in and spreading the shroud." They all bore him to tears apart from the night nurse, who laughs at his dirty jokes. He doesn't do anything nowadays. Some crosswords, some of *Le Figaro*, some radio, some music, no TV. He's bored stiff. He doesn't see the point of being an old man anymore. During the first months that he was immobilized, he was obsessed with the idea of ending it all. He took stock of his sorry state, his diapers, his catheter. He begged me to mix him a lethal cocktail. He used his phone with super-huge print and left me multiple messages a week to that effect. I gave it serious thought; I made a few calls that came to naught apart from the Belgian solution. But such an official solution would have required the approval of his son, who lives in Boston, and Maurice categorically refused to let him know. Maurice has always had issues with this son. I remember him as a teenager, a grumpy, ill-at-ease figure who looked down on us. During his wedding in Tel Aviv to a nice beautiful Sabra, the two fathers, on edge, went into a back room to work out the costs of the reception.

Maurice said, "We're here to get fleeced and your girl's just marrying my boy for my money."

"Why else would she marry him," the other father retorted, "with that head on his shoulders?"

The marriage lasted mere months and the divorce cost Maurice a fortune. The son had moved to Massachusetts afterward, only to insist that he get to run his father's life from five thousand kilometers away.

Maurice strikes me as more relaxed lately. Not too long ago I found out that he's been eating with more appetite and seeing the physical therapist three times a week. They make it to the living room together, where they go around the ugly red corduroy sofa with the IV stand and the urine bag.

Maurice hates this stroll and hates the physical therapist.

I say, "If you're so keen on dying, why are you seeing the physical therapist three times a week?"

He answers, "Well, since I don't know if you're going to do something, I'm going for the better of the two options."

He did this to me once before, a few years ago after heart surgery. He was put into a convalescent home and couldn't stand it. I didn't have the time to go there but I called him. "A convalescent home? It's a hovel, a gymnasium! You're in the physical therapists' lair and you don't see a single real doc. I can't get any sleep, I can't take a shit, the bathroom's a disgrace, they're making me move my legs with machines. I shouldn't have agreed to this. I shouldn't have agreed to the operation. I should have snuffed it in peace. I've had a nice life, what's left for me now?"

I said, "Get yourself out of there, Maurice. Talk to the guy running the place, tell him you're checking out."

"Yeah, yeah . . . but what if I'm making a stupid mistake with my health?"

"You just said you'd rather die."

He replied, "Yes, I'd rather die. But considering that I've made it this far . . ."

His dentures are sticking out. Constant canastas. He actually seems to be having fun with them.

After a minute, I've had enough. "Stop it with those dentures!"

Paulette, his second wife, slips into the room. She backs me up.

I say, "Those dentures need to be stuck back together, he looks senile."

She nods. "He should have gotten implants, naturally! The Blums got implants around eighty," she said. "I told Tamara her family was smart to get those implants young."

"But Albert's implants didn't take," Maurice says.

"No, those implants didn't take, poor soul. Tamara wanted to put him in one of those homes, because, now, naturally . . . The thing is, the only home she saw that she approved of is in Verdon-la-Forêt, an hour outside Paris. And, at her age, Tamara isn't driving anymore . . ."

"Who cares! Leave us be, Paulette."

"Do you remember your father fell out with Albert?" Paulette says to me.

"Oh, how come?"

"Because they were each bragging about introducing the other to Mahler's work. They came to blows!"

"Everyone knows that!" Maurice says.

"They never could come to terms. Just between you and me, Albert's right, no question of it. Edgar didn't know the first thing about music. Apart from the Symphony No. 5, what could he know of Mahler's? Tamara was completely on Albert's side. She knew your father had no ear and, broadly speaking, no artistic sensibility. For years, every time they saw each other Edgar would say: 'Spit your venom, Tamara! Go on, spit your venom!' She was a bit venomous, wasn't she . . ."

"Who cares, Paulette!"

"See what he puts me through," Paulette says as she leaves the room.

"All right, talk to me a bit. What's new? Did you see how she kept saying 'naturally' every ten seconds? Why don't you find yourself a nice girl? You're a handsome man."

"I've got my share of nice girls."

"Are you still seeing that Marion? She's a nice one."

"A very nice one."

"And the boy? How's he turning out? What's his name again?"

"Luc. Do you want me to put you back upright?"

"You can have a child too. Give me the control . . ."

"What control?"

"The fan control. I had a fan put in the ceiling. The same one as at Raffles. Did you see it? Did you see how beautiful those blades are?"

He presses the clicker several times; the blades start whirring and make a small gust of wind in the room.

"Really something, isn't it? . . . Give me that box there . . . The candy. Yes, there."

Slumped back, he holds out an impatient hand. I give him the box of pastilles that I unearth beneath magazines in an overfull compartment of the bedside table (also a medical one).

Not even trying to pull himself upright, he starts struggling to open it. I try to help him but he wants to do it himself. The box pops open and the black pastilles scatter all over the bed. "Shit!" I race to pick them up in the gust. His hand gropes blindly in the sheets for them and he wolfs them down.

He immediately begins coughing hollowly and terrifyingly. He's choking.

Paulette rushes in. "What's happened to him? Who gave him those pastilles? He can't have licorice!"

We get him upright. We slap his back.

"Stop that wind!"

He finally pukes up the candy in a slimy mess of drool and mucus.

"You want to die choking on licorice? Have it your way! Why'd you spit it out then? You had your solution right there!" Paulette says in her shrill voice while wiping his face. "You're the one who set the fan on high? I've had it with you."

She storms out, whispering an inaudible litany. Maurice's dazed for a minute and then he starts clacking his dentures again.

"I can't stand those chaperones."

"We're going to Auschwitz at the end of the month with Nana and Serge."

"To Auschwitz? What's wrong with you?"

"Joséphine's gotten it in her head to go ever since her grandmother's death. She'd like for her father to come along. Nana's fine with it and plans on coming. Serge's freaking out at the idea of being with those two. So I'm going too."

"That's no place!"

I shrug. It's a waste of time to opine on these developments.

"That's a surprise, coming from your brother."

"Valentina kicked him out."

"Was he an idiot?"

"Probably."

"Where's he now?"

"Seligmann, the guy managing his record store, lent him a furnished apartment by the Champ de Mars."

"She was a good one, that girl."

"Yes."

"You find a girl like that, you hang onto her. So, you're forking over money to those Polacks. What else are you doing at Auschwitz?"

"We'll see."

"Where did the idea come from?"

I grab the box of licorice and down three or four.

"I'm just with the band here."

"Start the fan again. It's stifling."

"Maman's family ended up there."

"If I got my legs back, that's the last place I'd go."

∾

Earlier in the year, Serge went to Switzerland for a cleanse. Valentina had been badgering him to do something about his weight, so he'd agreed to spend some time at a holistic clinic on Lake Vaar. There, breathing in the Waponitzberg air on his panoramic tiled balcony, bundled up in a sheepskin coat and swaddled in a blanket, he began a practically gold-plated *repos digestif* (in other words, a fast) with vegetable broth and mineral water. The next day, the broth was gone from the protocol; he was left with as much mineral water and fragrant tea as he wished. A feeling of sadness had overcome him, as all the perks of the cleanse—body wraps, meditation, yoga, life coaching, not to mention winter hikes—horrified him. Valentina had come along. Her presence had been no consolation, as she was on a standard diet and could sit in front of a white tablecloth and silverware at mealtimes. Not to mention that she indulged in all activities with infuriating zeal when she wasn't swanning around in a bathrobe at the Beauty Center. Serge spent his days between balcony and bed, glued to his phone, his glowing blue rectangle, his sole window to the normal world. On the fourth day, Valentina found him with a cigarette in his mouth, ban notwithstanding, dressed like a businessman and zipping shut his suitcase. Earlier in the morning she had been so bold as to congratulate him on vegetable broth being reintroduced.

On the way home she scolded him not for the rushed departure but for making a scene at the front desk. It appalled her that he'd been so crass and petty. Because of course there was no chance he would be reimbursed for the remainder of the week.

"Six thousand euros for celery broth! Those bastards! What a scam!" had been Serge's verdict as he drove at a breakneck pace. "It's a racket! See where all the bullshit in your women's magazines have gotten us? The front-desk guy was a Nazi! 'Sir, you signed the agreement!' The agreement! What fucking agreement? How am I supposed to know what I signed? I'm a fatass. I like my fat ass, I'm happy this way! And there are folks who *like* me fat! Know what we're going to do, Valentina? Find Zurbigën on the map. And I'll start with a beer, that'll open my pylorus right up!"

"Who likes you fat?"

"Folks. And I'm not fat, I'm bloated. I get bloated because I eat faster than a dog. Don't forget that. No pooch could beat me."

"What folks? Peggy Wigstrom?"

"What about her?"

"Peggy Wigstrom? That'd be vile, you know that?"

"Oh, come on!"

"Are you sleeping with Peggy Wigstrom?"

"Don't be ridiculous! Some help this cleanse has been for you."

"Answer the question!"

"I could be her father!"

"Since when has that stopped any man?"

"I don't know how you got this idea in your head, Valentina."

"You swear?"

"I swear to you! There's nothing between me and Peggy Wigstrom. I swear."

"On Joséphine's head?"

"On Joséphine's head."

That night, at the Walser House in Zurbigën, after devouring a French onion soup and then a pigeon breast stuffed with its thighs, Serge said to Valentina, "To be honest, *tesoro mio*, I don't buy all of these rules about dieting. It's possible, I think, to get thinner if you make up your mind to. And to shape a body by imagining it without having to work out. See, I turned down the bread! I'm entitled to a little dessert, aren't I?"

"Because folks like you fat?"

"Oh, *micetta*, you're so cruel."

The next day, on their way out from a dinner possibly even better than the previous night's, while pulling a choux off his St. Honoré cake with his bare fingers, an idea took root in Serge's head: here, in the Walser House's kitchens, and nowhere else, his nephew Victor could spend the following summer completing his apprenticeship as a chef. He waved down a maître d' and asked if Monsieur Popper, hoping to thank him personally, could meet the chef.

"Why don't you give Victor a call before you do that," Valentina suggested.

"He's been trying to line up a stage for the summer. How could he do better than this?"

"Did he say that?"

"Nana did."

"Call him anyway."

"Always complicating things! I'll text him. Here: 'Summer at the Walser House hotel, one of the best restaurants in Switzerland. Interested? Uncle Serge.'"

After some petits fours and Fernet, they left the dining room. At the back of the cavernous kitchens, the chef was waiting for them. A brown-haired, affable man who grew up in the alpine meadows of Waponitzberg and only spoke German and English. Availing himself of the latter language in his notorious accent, Serge started by saying that the chef deserved, at the very least, a Michelin star. After one or two further compliments, he introduced his nephew, Victor, in short, a stellar boy who loved cooking, just out of the famous École Émile Poillot and in search of a stage for the summer. The chef had never heard of the École Émile Poillot but graciously welcomed the query and suggested that the young man email him his CV.

"I did sound good, didn't I?" Serge asked in the gemütlich hallway leading to the bedroom they now had. He'd originally been given room eighteen: an unacceptable number. One plus eight equaled nine, the number of death. Serge had gotten a room change.

"You did sound very good."

"I did right to mention the Michelin star. He liked that."

"He seemed to."

Serge was convinced that numbers determined his fate. Once, in Cyprus, he'd changed his hotel room three times. The first had a bad number, the second, two adjoining beds that seemed like graves, the third a glaring brown-black bedspread. Whenever Serge left a room, the last thing his eyes saw ought to be a friendly object or a positive color. Black was negative. When he was stuck on a black thing, he had to immediately ward it off by fixating on something light two times in a row without any slipping up. It was exhausting. Not to mention the eyestrain.

"And I still haven't heard back from Victor," Serge added. "Just like his father. It's easier to talk with the Pope than the Ochoas."

∽

The Ochoas, father and son alike, both have outdated phones and it's impossible to get hold of them directly. There's that. But whereas the father's inertia is simply exasperating, the son's lack of interest is brazen and baffling. Most kids are physically attached to their phones, but not Victor. The boy can't be found on any of his generation's favorite social networks, and he only just got a cell phone with Internet. My nephew Victor Ochoa isn't like his father, to be clear. A teensy bit of good old Spanish pride, a smidge of hypersensitivity, sure, but that's about it. There's nothing Popper about him, in any case—as if there was anything consistent about Poppers! What I mean is he isn't any more like his mother, physically or temperamentally, considering that, over the years, she's clearly Ochoized herself.

He does get a kick out of driving her mad in the kitchen, even though Nana's always considered herself a genius at the stove. Whenever he bothers to stop by his parents' (thankfully not often, now that he lives with roommates from school), he's a backseat driver. "Why are you boiling the meat and not searing it?" "Why are you burning the sauce already when you haven't even cooked the pasta yet?" "Why are you letting the mushrooms soak up all the water?" "If you'd just stick your green vegetables in an ice bath right after cooking them then you wouldn't be serving khaki vegetables to your guests." "Salsify? In May?" The more he criticizes her, the more she messes things up. She second-guesses herself and doesn't know what she's doing anymore. One day she was cutting an onion with a bread knife and Victor said, "Oh, I can't wait to see you cut bread with a mandoline!" and she pointed the long, serrated blade at him.

The next day, Victor called Serge as he was driving; Valentina held the phone to his mouth with the speaker on. "Send him an email, in English," Serge shouted, "tell him what dates work for you, your degree, your previous experience and where you worked, that thing at Arcachon Bay where you graduated to meat after two weeks, Le Meurice, *tutti quanti*." Victor thanked him unenthusiastically and promised to send the email that evening.

"He's not surprised," Serge said to Valentina once they'd hung up.

"It's not surprising. You're his uncle."

"That I am."

Back in Paris, Serge bragged to Nana that he'd sorted out her son's summer at a first-rate spot. "And the best part is," he added, "he'll be in a spot to die for: the Swiss Alps. He does love to travel."

Nana thanked him warmly.

∼

Whenever I get back home, there isn't anyone expecting me. I never say "It's me!" with that upbeat tone I've heard in some houses; I never expect a "hellooooo" back or the patter of footsteps. I haven't set my life up for that, but I still feel stupid when I catch myself suddenly nostalgic for a bustling house, coziness, stretches of time that become ritual even just for routine chores. How can I keep from getting stuck in such ruminations? When I was younger I loved that song about all the boys in the world deciding to be friends. For ages I figured things would play out like that, and a little part of me still does: clean-cut boys walking arm in arm, a brotherly rank of stout souls, of jacks-of-all-trades. Of course, we weren't stuck with wives or families. I could sneak off to the tent every so often with a girl while the others kept on singing around the fire (and never fucked). But no love affairs, no children, none of those burdens on the horizon.

Marion thinks there's nothing odd about telling me about her relationship. I don't know how I've ended up being her confidant. In theory, a man with his wits about him would have nipped this in the bud, before any bitter cracks of disappointment grew. That sap's giddier than I've ever seen her. Everything's got her overjoyed. As for me, everything's got to be a new way to needle her.

She tells me that her guy was born in Buenos Aires, where he spent several years.

"How come you're saying Bwayy-nos Ayy-rrress?"

"Because it's nice."

"You don't say Mayyyn-hhhhattan."

"No. But I say Bwayy-nos Ayy-rrress. So what?"

"I care!"

"You just might be going crazy."

"How come you're saying Bwayy-nos Ayy-rrress in the middle of a sentence in French."

"Because I like it. So there!"

"So wrong. You're saying Bwayy-nos Ayy-rrress because you're imitating him."

"Well, what if I am?"

"That's not like you."

"Are you jealous?"

"You are. You're crazy too, Marion."

Two years ago, I took her and Luc to Venice. I rented a one-bedroom by the Frari. The three of us together worked out nicely. On Easter Monday, we hurried down the street, worried the grocery store would be closing early. We saw a Black beggar and Marion stopped; I said in Italian that we'd come back. When we did come back, all I had was my credit card and Marion had two bills. The guy said, "*Puoi cambiare*?" and Marion wanted to go back to the store to get some change. There was a huge line at checkout. The clerk told her he was all out, pointing at his cash drawer. All the other shops nearby were closed.

Marion said, "I don't dare to walk past that beggar again," so we took a different route, but she was upset. "I feel bad for the man, it's wrong to make a promise and not keep it."

I said, "He'll be fine."

"He's waiting for us. If we don't come back, how is that going to make life look any better for him?"

"You're overthinking it, Marion." The grocery bag was heavy.

"The cashier said he was all out but he didn't actually show us. We could have gotten some change by buying some little knickknack."

"But you saw how ugly they were. Nothing under five euros, either!"

We crossed a bridge and found ourselves in front of a store selling postcards and Marion raced in to buy one. She had the change. Luc wanted to go back too. We retraced our steps with all the tourists coming the other way and the grocery bag, which had to weigh ten tons. The beggar recognized us and wished us a *Buona Pasqua* with a polite smile.

"See, we did the right thing to come back!" Marion said. But, a few meters on, she was glowering again. "I can't stand it that he probably thought we gave him money because it was Easter."

In any case, I'm more or less crucified by this grotesque romance with the guy from Argentina. I hadn't imagined Marion could have this sort of grip on me. Lately, anything out of the ordinary gets to me. On the high-speed train I saw a magazine with a terrifying photo of Céline Dion on the cover. She'd become a brunette with short, greasy hair cut into a pen nib across her forehead. She was crouching in an insane pose, her legs spread in too-big jeans, her feet in pointy-toed ankle boots. The lady looked like she was in pure hell. She's drowning in that horrific neon-green track jacket, I thought, and in all that marketing. I felt sad. Not for her, but for the way the world had changed. The men of my generation were sinking into drugs and fantasies. For better or worse, they stayed real while we found something to dream about. To get hold of myself I cast my mind on Auschwitz. Where not a single one of these vague wishes could waft up. If I start thinking about Auschwitz (usually I wouldn't take such drastic measures), it's because Joséphine, that spry thing in need of some sort of identity, is all too keen to tread on the graves of her forefathers and drag along the whole motley crew of us unthinking, unbothered souls—her father, her aunt, and me, her uncle.

∽

On Carole's orders, Serge had gone to the end-of-school performances at Joséphine's dance school. Each year, he watched his chubby, crabby girl clumsily follow the choreography in an ill-fitting leotard. And he got into the doldrums. The other parents filmed, clapped, and rushed over to their kids in a cheerful hubbub, while he waited in the back, bent over a stool, unable to say a single nice thing when the little girl popped up with her crinkled, worried face. In short, he felt cursed.

This girl never did manage to be the sweet lissome vine her father dreamed of. Let alone the genius he'd merely hoped for. Joséphine simply plodded along from one year to the next without much protest. When she was fifteen she got kicked out for skipping too many classes and forging parent signatures. After some further attempts at schooling, she took a shine to cosmetology, which her father deemed a sad excuse for a career even as he forced himself to go on writing checks for private school anyway. For a while she was swanning around for perfume chains (*swanning*! as if I've been trotting out that word forever without ever quite getting what it means) until she found herself in the security office at the Champs-Élysées Sephora, being called a petty thief. Nowadays she styles herself as a makeup artist and makes her living as a contractor for TV shows. Maybe I should give Joséphine more credit, though. I don't actually know all that much about her, apart from Serge's rants and those family lunches where nobody's at their best.

This year, whether out of some fatherly regret or some organ degenerating, my brother decided two things pertaining to his daughter: to go with her to Poland, and to buy her a studio. Given Serge's finances, Valentina offered to be the guarantor. Rather thoughtful and noble, considering how little effort Joséphine was putting in. Joséphine was the one to start looking around. Their first visit, a seventh-floor studio on rue Poulet right by boulevard Barbès, convinced my brother to take matters into his own hands. "An attic room in the Arab neighborhood, that's all she could find!" Valentina pointed him to an energetic real-estate agent who, according to her, had a solid contact list: she'd gotten Valentina her own apartment. A certain Peggy Wigstrom. A pretty blonde thirtysomething with such an immaculate chignon that, the one time I saw her, I imagined her to have an array of riding crops. Did Serge have the same thought? He really did take this apartment search to heart, visiting places even without Joséphine, who in any case wouldn't have set foot in the fusty *quartiers* that her father wanted to put her up in.

One day, aware that he was on the phone with Peggy Wigstrom, Valentina heard him let out a funny laugh. A fake, stupid, bawdy laugh.

"What's so funny?"

"Funny?"

"You were practically bent over laughing."

"Oh, no, nothing at all. She just found another spot by Auteuil—can you imagine Joséphine seeing it?!"

"You're so stupid when you're trying to be charming."

"All men are stupid, *tesoro mio*."

"You aren't getting a bit fond of this gal, are you?"

"Of course not!"

Peggy Wigstrom lurked quietly in the back of each of their minds until the road to Zurbigën, where all it took was an ill-timed remark to bring her right to the fore. But Serge had sworn. Sworn on his daughter's head that he wasn't sleeping with Peggy Wigstrom. She'd believed him. You don't swear on the head of your own daughter if you don't mean it. It boggled the mind that women had always been so gullible.

Since the dawn of time, men have said all sorts of things. Men never bother to stand by their words. Words are meaningless to them. Utter them and they float away like bubbles that burst ever so gently in the air. Who pays them any heed? If something goes wrong, that can be fixed with a few more words that float away in turn, and so on. "Swear on Joséphine's head," Valentina had said. "On Joséphine's head," Serge had said without missing a beat, and maybe even with a touch of hurt, before not losing any sleep over it and not bringing it to any purifying Golgotha of sorts. Valentina had believed him. The night was saved, and Peggy Wigstrom retreated back into the shadows.

∽

Buying a place is no mean feat. Like it or not, there's a life-and-death aspect to the matter. Wigstrom aside, Serge visits these studios imagining that it's he, in tatters and cast out by all, who will while away the rest of his time on earth there. A studio meant to avail the owner and the tenant is the fundamental principle of real estate, though. But what criteria could possibly be shared by two souls so existentially unlike one another? Joséphine doesn't mind stairs, loves the hustle and bustle and bars and métros, while her father's priorities are elevators and doorways and bathrooms wide enough for a walker, generously proportioned hallways, a peaceful neighborhood with a brasserie for lunches and watching pretty girls go by. Every so often one of us has to remind Serge that this studio isn't an antecrypt meant to house him. He knows it. But he doesn't understand his daughter, he doesn't understand her choices. What sort of man is he to get into someone else's head? When he's up for it he goes with her to the Oberkampf, his body plodding yet intrepid, and forces himself to look for positive signs—a nice street number, a welcoming color in the hall, not a single darkened storefront shutter in sight.

Yesterday, on rue Honoré-Pain, I saw a pigeon fall onto the road. It lay on its back, its wings flapping for a few seconds. Then it was dead. Up above, gathered on an awning, a group of other pigeons looked on. I wondered what they felt. Did they shove it? This morning, a few meters from my place, in a corner of rue Grèze which intersects rue Honoré-Pain, a crow was pecking ravenously at the dead pigeon, which was now several meters over and no longer had a head. I stopped to observe the gleaming creature at its job. I thought of Serge, for whom such a sight at the foot of his door would have aroused mortal anguish. With a sharp movement, the crow turned its neck to me, staring at me with its yellow eyes full of scorn: "My street, my loot. My rue Grèze, a wilderness." I gave it a ridiculously wide berth as I walked to my door. I looked down. Yes, Mister Crow.

I was reminded of a scene in *The Brothers Karamazov*: a man whipping a horse across its docile eyes. Other translations say its *sweet* eyes. But *docile* elevates the sentence.

∾

"Maman's depressed in the morning, scowling at noon, the life of the party at night." This quip of Margot's lingers in my mind as I call her mother in the late afternoon. Sure enough, I catch her on the way to merriment. Nana's overseeing our trip to Auschwitz. She volunteered herself as a pro (she's been a coordinator for four years now at a charity connected with the childcare system—she sets up family vacations for the impoverished). She gives me the rundown like a perfect secretary: flights booked and boarding passes printed; hotel reservations set up right by the camp; nine o'clock slot selected for the Polish guided tour of the Memorial.

"Polish?"

"Yep. That's the only way to get in that day. There were no more spaces for self-guided visitors. But we'll break off from the group right away. You'll figure out the car?"

"It's taken care of already."

"I'd love to have brought Margot. But she has the baccalaureate this year."

"We're not making a delegation visit of it."

"She almost got to go with her class in December, but she didn't make the cut."

"Thank God!"

"Why?"

"I'm kidding."

"Ah, yes. Haha. Ask her about it, you'll be laughing."

"Laughing?"

"Yes, yes. You'll see. What's the latest with Serge?"

"He's not doing great."

"You don't think she left him for good, do you?"

"It's a rough patch, but they've been through those before."

"That'd be the stupidest mistake he'd ever made. She's really something special, that Valentina. He'll never find another girl like her."

"That's true."

"Is there anything we can do?"

"Like what?"

"Hey, apparently the Swiss chef never got back to Victor!"

"Is that so? You should tell Serge."

"Victor sent over his CV, his references, all of it, in English, nice and proper. It's been two months now. You know they figure those things out way in advance."

"So tell Serge."

"But if he's already hit rock bottom . . ."

"He could make another call."

"Yes . . . It really would be lovely for Victor to spend the summer at the Walser."

"So tell Serge to follow up."

"Yes . . ."

"He's the one you should be talking to, not me!"

"Yes, okay, I'll do it."

Could it be that Valentina had left Serge for good?

Valentina's way out of Serge's league. As far as we can tell what his league is. They've been together for five years. Serge met her at the office of the lawyer who defended Jacky Alcan in the carbon tax affair (Jacky had been recruiting shell managers for shell companies). Nobody could have predicted that this sharp, put-together woman, a senior executive at Lactalis, might fall for someone like Serge.

Could it be that she had actually left him? I hadn't imagined things in such terms just yet.

Yes, losing Valentina would be a massive mistake.

∽

On a temperate February evening, about a month after their Swiss expedition, Valentina happened to see a message on Serge's phone: *Call me on the other one*. The device was right there, still unlocked. Who had those words gone flying to? Why was it in writing? The words floated on the white background; the preceding conversation seemed to have been erased. Much as the contours of familiar things—every sign of joy and trust— had now been erased.

When Serge walked back into the room, what he saw was a livid, bristling woman.

"Where's the other one?"

"The other what?"

"The other phone, you piece of shit!"

"What are you talking about, Va—"

He didn't even get a chance to say her whole name; she'd pounced on him, rummaged through his pockets, knocked him over, unearthed the unobtrusive Wiko, and thrown it across the room.

"Get the hell out! Get the hell out of here! You and that bitch I personally introduced you to! *Personally!*"

She was screaming, hitting him, opening a cabinet, pulling his belongings out of drawers, yanking belts and shirts and jackets off of hangers and tossing them on the ground.

"Where's that suitcase, you asshole? Go find it before I end you!"

In the bathroom she threw out razors, shaving cream, toothbrushes, cologne. Serge tried to get hold of her and calm her down, but Valentina was already ransacking a shelf in the bedroom. There was no stopping a woman like her on the warpath.

"On your daughter's head! You swore on your daughter's head! . . . And don't get me started on Wigstrom, that Kraut with fake boobs . . ."

"Not Ganesha! Not my Ganesha!"

"Of course you'd fuck a Kraut, Jews love their Germans."

"Valentina!"

"Don't 'Valentina' me!"

He got under the desk and grabbed the terra-cotta dancing Ganesha figurine that a medium in Auroville had given him. Valentina went into the entryway with a stepladder. Standing on it, she hauled down the black suitcase I've known since time immemorial. She stuffed it with everything she'd grabbed—he was forced to help her so she didn't leave a mess everywhere.

"I don't care if you're fucking sluts left and right, men don't know what the hell to do with their dicks, but don't you lie to me! Don't you dare lie to me! Don't you disrespect me like that!

I never looked at your messages, I never tracked you. I trusted you, and what do I get for it, what does this good, honest idiot who believes everything get for it? You scum, buying your little Wiko like a coward and sleeping with that slut of a real estate agent helping you find an apartment for your daughter. A slut I personally introduced you to. And you told me on the drive from the Walser that *I* was crazy? I have never been so humiliated! So completely humiliated!"

"Don't be like all those girls nowadays, Valentina!"

"All those girls nowadays spit on you! Where's your stupid little thing gone?"

She dug through the suitcase, found the guardian Ganesha that he thought was safe and sound deep in a sleeve, and threw it as hard as she could onto the kitchen tiles. The figurine shattered. Serge contemplated the god in ruins. After a second of shock and horror, he crouched down to hurriedly gather the shards, all of them, even the smallest ones, even the dust on the ground, which he deposited on a dish towel. And then he was reminded once again of those dark thoughts he'd had on their first night in room twenty-five at the Walser House. Valentina had been asleep, snug against his body while his eyes had bored into the darkness. What had he done, swearing on the head of his daughter? Had he brought doom upon the child? In his thoughts had been a vague image of snakes coiling around the legs of the person in question. How could he take back those reckless words? They'd come in the heat of the moment—what were they, chopped liver? Something had to be done so nothing could befall Joséphine. He'd need to pull quite a few rabbits out of a hat here. Yes. He'd have to pull off even more of his stratagems (plenty of which I haven't mentioned yet, never mind the ones I still don't know about). He'd have to go and do all sorts of mitzvot. He recalled seeing Red Cross volunteers going around one evening by the Vaugirard cemetery. I'll sign up at the local office, he decided, I'll go out at night wearing that orange parka and pushing that cart, I'll hand out warm soup, paper and pencils, a toiletry kit, he'd thought with a twinge of emotion. Yes, I will. Two times at least, he'd promised himself. And now, on all fours in the kitchen, as he rummaged around on the tiles, he felt like a tremendous weight had been taken off his shoulders. I'm being punished, he thought, I, Serge Popper, am being punished, I and not my innocent daughter! Which was why he so carefully gathered up the Ganesha in shards, certain of this blemished god's continuing strength and mercy.

In a rather cold voice, he'd told Valentina as he got up: "You poor thing, you're completely insane."

Valentina kicked the suitcase toward the door.

"Let me close it!"

He saw the Wiko by a plinth. Valentina beat him to it. They struggled; he managed to pry it out of her hands and throw it out the window. She started sobbing.

"Why do I have to live a life like this? Whatever did I do to God to deserve all this?"

He zipped the suitcase and shoved it onto the landing.

"*Ciao*. I'm out of your hair now. I'm free!"

∽

That same evening, I set him up in my home office, where Luc sleeps when Marion leaves him with me, and I took him to the street-level bistro for some lamb cutlets. He struck me as having his mind all over the place but generally being all right.

"Valentina wears cologne," he said. A particular brand, I'd forgotten about that. "The smell reminds her of her parents. Emigrants from Calabria—he was a mason. You'd walk by folks with that scent by rue Bredaine, with their hair brushed back, threadbare shirts buttoned all the way up to the neck. But I don't care. She's crazy. You're right. No getting married. No scenes, no jealousy. That Italian lady is the worst, she won't be swayed. She gets herself all worked up, there's no talking sense into her. Even she, the one who's a cut above all the rest, isn't a cut above all the rest. You think she's smart, but she's just a walking bag of hormones like the rest of them. Last night I got to the hereafter, and they were saying, 'Your father's in heaven with a north-facing room, your mother's in hell and facing south with a whole Sri Lankan staff.' What do you make of that? The Montrouge lot is dead in the water. Chicheportiche had the mayor in his pocket, so nobody can get a permit to build even one floor higher. We'll have to sell it at a loss."

By the end of the dinner, after two bottles of a top-notch Saint-Julien, we've deciphered, through the screen of the three-quarters-wrecked Wiko, his conversation with Peggy Wigstrom. Half sweetness and half smuttiness. *Slave awaits depraved Valkyrie. Come with your wings of steel. Your faithful dog.* Or, in the same vein, *Are your tits as perky as the peaks of your hat? Spread wide, Thor's coming to dominate you.* We cried with laughter at *Thor's coming to dominate you*, and also at the thought of Valentina's head, had the phone ended up in her hands after all.

The next morning, I found him sitting at the end of the bed, dazed and gloomy in his underwear. On the dresser was a blister pack of Xénotran that he must have been chipping away at through the night. He'd tried to call Valentina over and over since sunup, but to no avail.

"Want some coffee?"

"I've been up since five. My sleep mask's still at the apartment."

"I'm headed to Provins for two days. Here, have the keys."

"You're leaving me here on my own?"

"I'll be back tomorrow night."

"What's the name of that property manager who's ripping me off? I can't for the life of me remember it."

"Patrick Seligmann."

"Ah, yes. Seligmann. His mother rents furnished places. He's the one I know, though—why can't I remember his last name? You think it's Alzheimer's?"

"It's happened to me, too. You're gonna rent a place?"

"Maybe he'll loan me one. Which will just prove me right that he's ripping me off. Alzheimer's, that'd be such a pain in the ass . . . Which organ's gonna go first? I'm on tenterhooks!"

He picked up one of the chestnuts that Luc had painted. Every fall, Luc collects chestnuts and draws faces on the lighter part. Eyes, nose, mouth.

"Why's he pouting?"

I opened a drawer and showed him my whole collection of painted chestnuts.

"I've got a few smilers here."

I laid them out on the wood chessboard that used to be our father's.

Serge asked, "Do you play sometimes?"

"When I'm back, I'll crush you."

"I'll crush you."

"Get yourself ready."

"When I can't take care of myself anymore," he says, bent over even more, "when I'm in some geriatric ward hallway, at the mercy of bitches handing me slices of toast at five in the morning, I won't let anyone come see me. I want to know I've been abandoned, not one bit of hope of any kind, nothing."

"I'll be back tomorrow night. Serge, it'll all work out."

"Nothing will work out. It's all a mess. I was unbreakable. And now it's all a mess."

"Want a chestnut?"

"Sure."

"Not one pouting!"

"Yes, one that's pouting."

"Fine. Here, take it."

I got the feeling he was broke. So I left him a bit of money too.

∾

There's something touching about the posture of a man sitting at the end of a bed. Shoulders slumped, chest sagging. Beds aren't made for such situations. A Hopper painting shows an almost fully dressed man in this indecisive moment. His hands dangle between his legs; he stares at the floor. Behind him, although it's not immediately noticeable, is a half-naked woman asleep and facing the wall. When I think of that image I don't remember her: the man is on his own, a loneliness that's just as visible by day as by night, that's nothing like other presences, the light, the décor. The loneliness is the bed and the weary pose. It's the wait for nothing. Nobody sees the man. The unobserved body accedes to despondency. This oddity of being unseen by anyone is reminiscent of childhood, of the possibility that the future might be empty. My brother, who had always been such a big presence, was suddenly smaller now. I left him in his underwear, slumped at the end of the bed, holding the chestnut with a pout. It occurred to me that I had some vague responsibility to him. I'm stronger than him now; I should watch over him.

∾

In Louan-Villegruis-Fontaine, around two in the morning, we were half-drunk and making our way into the woods with Bruno Bourboulon, a colleague from the control center, when I got a call from Serge. Valentina had texted him that she'd dumped the rest of his belongings into an IKEA bag, which he could come and pick up by the trash if he got there before the garbagemen did. Serge had immediately headed for rue Trichet, where the bag was lying in the hutch, ready to be taken. He thought about going upstairs and ringing the bell, but he didn't dare because of Marzio. I didn't really get what it was he wanted or what I could do from so far off, especially since we were wandering aimlessly in a damp chill with a mini flashlight to find our "cottage"—an RV. Bourboulon had jumped practically naked into the heated pool, he was still dripping and had started moaning even as he was humming "Les Lacs du Connemara." I told Serge to go back to my place and to let it go.

"When I look in the mirror," I could barely hear him saying over the traffic, "when I see my funereal blotches, my subdued eyes, my faux-limp strands of hair in the running, I think to myself how much time you've got left . . . Taxi! . . . Taxi! . . . They've got green lights on and they won't stop for you! . . . I've hit rock bottom here, no apartment, a hobo bag. Seligmann could just give me a mousehole with a courtyard right by the Champ de Mars. Stick me in the Champ de Mars for just two days and I'll hang myself."

"Of course."

"You know old age is overnight? Overnight. One day you wake up and you can't pull yourself together anymore, old age's got you by the throat . . ."

"Serge, go back to my place, take a long shower. I'll be there tomorrow night, we'll talk then. Serge . . . ?"

I couldn't hear anything now.

"Serge . . . ?"

What was I doing in this no-man's-land with Bourboulon? The next day I had a guided tour of Province and a railbike trip. I could have been in the archery group, but no, I was in the railbike group. I tried to call Serge back. His phone battery must be dead. Finally, we found our "cottage." I couldn't possibly get to sleep. At the end of the musical evening, Bourboulon had done the paquito with the IT project manager and the guy from Enercoop who'd come to brag all about the social impact. I'd drunk far too much and, like an idiot, laughed far too much. I examined the prefab room. I missed those small seaside hotels when we did low-key department outings. I pulled out my iPad and watched the last episode of *Narcos: Mexico*.

At the end, before everything blows up, Neto asks Miguel Félix Gallardo why he got into coke.

"We had a good thing with the weed. And it could have gone forever, but it wasn't enough for you."

"We had to expand."

"We had to expand," Neto repeats. "Really?"

I have a friend from my year who went on to start a line of kitchens. He's talking about opening a store in Hamburg. He's just made it in Paris and he's already plotting to take over Europe. My friends keep changing jobs and each time they change jobs they say they should have done it a year earlier. And you're still in the same old place. A big fish in a small pond.

The next day, Serge texted me to say that he was off to live in Seligmann's place. I got the message on the bus taking us to Nation. All was quiet; everyone was wiped out. Plenty of them still had another hour of travel to get home. I sent Marion a picture of me clowning around with my colleagues on a railbike so she'd show Luc. The bus made me think of our upcoming trip to Poland, and Margot's story.

Margot Ochoa's tale:

In the fall our philosophy teacher, Monsieur Cerezo, an overburdened Jew, signed our class up for a competition set up by the Shoah Memorial in Paris. We had to give a presentation on a topic of our choice related to the concentration camps. First prize would be a class trip to Auschwitz. I was picked along with two other girls to give the presentation and we won the prize. The class trip could only be fifteen students. There were thirty of us. Monsieur Cerezo decided that the fifteen would be chosen at random. We had to write our names on a small piece of paper (except for Prune Mirza, who didn't think she was humanly capable of going there and whose sorrow commanded such sympathy from Monsieur Cerezo: "Do you really think the ones being sent there felt any more capable?"). The pieces of paper were put in a hat, then pulled out by the innocent hand of Flore Alouche. Neither I nor my two friends were picked, which felt really unfair. At five in the morning, standing in front of the school, the chosen ones got onto the bus for the airport. Monsieur Cerezo was on the trip, of course, as well as Madame Hainaut, the geography and history teacher. On the road, the mood was somewhat boisterous—part excitement, part exhaustion. At place Champerret, Monsieur Cerezo made it clear that everyone was not only to calm down but also to take up an attitude of sorrowful contemplation in keeping with the circumstances. Some immediately put on a mask of suffering without even wondering if they might have to maintain it unvaryingly for forty-eight hours. Since, to hear our friends, there was no getting past Monsieur Cerezo's watchful eye. At the entrance to Auschwitz, as the students queued in front of the main gate, he stood right by the guide to stare at the faces and make sure that each one looked suitably horrified. He also punctuated each detail given by the guide with a sad nod. When one student was so unlucky as to speak to another in a voice that wasn't a despairing whisper or even just to relax their face, Monsieur Cerezo suddenly appeared. Solène Mazamet thought she might be able to hint to her friend that she was cold (in mid-December in Poland). "Oh, are you cold, my poor Solène? Just imagine. Imagine how cold those souls who were undressed in this very spot might have been, who stayed standing and unmoving for hours in the snow, without any food, without any sleep. Solène, frozen and naked before they were gassed!" If he saw a cell phone emerge (he had banned them) or thought he heard a snicker, he threatened to send the offender back to the meeting spot in the parking lot. Madame Hainaut, every bit as terrorized, made her way like a shadow along the buildings. On the second day of this reign, as he stood at the top of the steps of a crematorium and after having listened, head bowed, to the guide's words, Monsieur Cerezo clarified with a sepulchral voice: "They were flogged with bullwhips." At those mere words, which were followed by others just as morose and theatrical, Madame Hainaut suddenly burst out laughing. A fit of laughter that she immediately tried to stifle with her scarf and transform into a fit of coughing, but the harder she tried to disguise it the more she snorted, to the point that, at the stairs to the crematorium, the whole group was now laughing. Stunned, suddenly speechless, nostrils flaring and puffing, Monsieur Cerezo finally said: "Well, I don't think there's anything I can do for you now. Congratulations, Madame Hainaut." And, sliding his bag over his anorak, he headed into the fog. They saw him head down the railroad tracks toward the camp entrance. At the end of the day, they found him sitting in the front of the bus, on the driver's side, mute and unreachable. Monsieur Cerezo didn't open his mouth again until Paris.

I felt oddly sad to find the apartment empty, oddly sad that he'd left so quickly. He's always been like that, I thought. Always better off elsewhere, even in that mousehole of Seligmann's. Why wasn't I just as ready to up and go, to leave places and people behind? We didn't even get to play chess. It's been years since we've played each other. I knew he'd played with others—could he maybe beat me now? In the more or less meaningful morass of images we still have of the past, chess has been a constant, fundamental motif. Our father had more quips than I could count about chess. One being "the king of games and game of kings." He was obsessed. He claimed to be a national master, well, national-master level. He subscribed to *Europe Échecs* and cut out studies or *Le Monde* chess puzzles. Every Sunday he could be seen in a pajama top, barefoot and balls dangling, wandering through the apartment with newspaper clippings and his magnetic travel chess set with small flat playing pieces, waiting for his glycerin suppository to kick in. He ended up on the toilet, where he would summon Serge (and, later, me) to finish the study of the game. Serge would sit uncomfortably on the bathtub rim and get an eyeful of all the father's intellectual and physiological exertions. They studied the games played by Spassky, Fischer, Capablanca, Steinitz, and others—but his hero, the man whose nobleness and boldness he never tired of praising, was Mikhail Tal, the genius of sacrifices, the Alexander the Great of the sixty-four squares. All these Russian and Czech champions were Jewish, he told us. And when the guy wasn't Jewish, he was still a Jew anyway. Of course we played. Against him at first, on the big chessboard now at my place. When we were little, he gave us a piece to start with, a rook, then a knight as we improved. Serge began to play well. My father didn't give him any more pieces. As soon as he sensed he was in danger, he would say, "Oh, how interesting, this situation really is interesting! Let's consider the variations!" He would upend the game being studied, it would become completely neutral, and nobody would win it now. Serge got annoyed. He insisted on real games. One day he actually won. "Check and mate," Serge said calmly, and he leaned back in his wingback chair, spreading his arms. My father reacted as if he'd been punched in the chest. "Oh, my little guy, you're a comedian all of a sudden, I gave you three moves, I told you how not to lose your queen! This guy here thinks he's actually won! A bit of modesty now, a bit of modesty, my little guy, if that's how you win then you're doomed for life!" At our place, losing at chess was a bloody humiliation. It was death. You went to war and you died. When Serge and I started playing each other, safe from a father who ruined games with his advice and commentary, the same hostility, the same dishonesty flared up in each of us. I had more focus than Serge. When I won, I was just a nasty little shit who'd gotten lucky when he'd lost his concentration for a second.

Now that I was back from Louan-Villegruis-Fontaine, I was sad that he was gone. I didn't even try to call him.

∽

It's hard to tell apart a relevant emotion and a brain malfunction. I proved that again by watching *Fauda*; seeing a 4×4 lurching through the desert and a herd of goats in the Golan Heights set off an uncomfortable wave of nostalgia. In other words, a sensation of having wrecked my real life. The same phenomenon arose with a report on a group of Moldavian poets living in low-rise buildings in Chisinau, and again in front of a country nurse showing us around her garden and explaining to the camera about the marjoram that René had given her, Marie-Jo's celery, even as a hen strutted through the foreground. The fact that "my real life" can take on such different forms oddly only reinforces the feeling of failure that sometimes overcomes me and that I've always told myself not to try to parse. How far can we trust its melancholies? When we turn our attention to what's going on in our skull, to all these forking paths, these interconnections of neurons and synapses, it's not so strange to attribute some states of mind to purely electrochemical reactions.

Cousin Maurice had an attack. The physical therapist showed up one morning. He leaned over the bed and immediately noticed slight facial paralysis. The doctor was summoned and she diagnosed it as a stroke; she had an IV put in and prescribed blood thinners. After a brief stretch of aphasia, Maurice started talking in an unfamiliar language that vaguely resembled Arabic while his right leg quivered nonstop.

"If we want to actually figure out what's going on," the doctor said, "he has to go to the hospital and get scanned, but he's a hundred years old, there's no getting him out of here."

After a few horrified confabs, the pool of women at his bedside came to agree with this assessment.

"It's no laughing matter," Paulette sighs as she opens the door for me. "Don't expect him to recognize you."

In the bedroom, she shouts in her shrill voice, "Maurice, it's Jean, Jean's here to see you!" She whispers to me, "He doesn't have his hearing aids in, we're not putting in his hearing aids while he's like this, naturally."

I look at his hands on the sheet. Those thin, veiny hands, old faithful friends, idle upon the cloth. I take one hand in mine. It's cold. I rub the fingers with mine. I gently massage this velveteen skeleton.

∾

"I talked to Serge," Nana told me a few days after our previous conversation. Her flat-timbered "I talked to Serge" with a trickle of air at the end immediately had me on edge. "He isn't well," she said (implying: the poor thing didn't say it but I can tell). "He really fucked up with Valentina" (translation: someday you'll understand, there are things a woman will never put up with). "He's scrounging for money" (meaning: of course, we ourselves can't be of any help, but maybe you . . . ?) "But he's so sweet, he still found time to send that chef at the Walser an email about Victor" (subtext: I'm so touched that he'd do that for his nephew considering his situation, you could even call him a family man).

Why did that all have me so on edge? Why? Is it her tone—how controlled and prudish her tone is—or how trite her understanding of the world? Ever since my sister got involved with giving back to the community, that mind of hers, which Ramos had already swallowed, became even blander.

When I look at Nana, I try to make out the young girl she used to be. I look in her eyes, in her body's movements, her laugh, even in her hair—in the whole assemblage that constitutes a being—for the traces of Anne Popper, the magic flower that her brothers revealed little by little at parties for self-aggrandizement. I make out nothing. Some people change in nature. Something happens that has nothing to do with life circumstances. Nor with old age or an organic catastrophe. It's a gradual change in substance that's beyond science. Nana managed to hoodwink my father, who paid for all sorts of schools, speech therapy, interior design—she sailed through with a charming nonchalance from one path to the next. Didn't she pursue law as well? She was seen taking drags on long American cigarettes and pretending to sulk with her hair tossed back on one side. She was invited to Jewish get-togethers; she's the only one of us three who had a little group of Jewish friends as a teen. "Looking for a dentist," Serge used to say in English. My father would have rather had her in the Israeli army, but a rich husband was also an option. And then the unthinkable happened. That elementary attraction which usually upends family expectations unexpectedly turned up Ramos Ochoa. A left-wing Spaniard from a Catholic *and* working-class background. I should point out that, at first, Serge and I didn't outright encourage—no, not that word!—but we did approve, maybe even applaud the arrival of this boy in a bandana (he wore a bandana and several bracelets), who was such a contrast with the gaggle of nice Jewish boys eyeing her up.

Early on, the Ramos guy was nice enough, kind of dull, with some Maoist stiffness softened by loving wonder. We didn't really care about him but we were drawn in by the sense of novelty that this crush brought out. That Nana had the nerve to get tangled up with someone named Ramos Ochoa made her sexy. My mother welcomed Ramos with open arms. They even went so far as to run down the lists of toreadors' names. My father was at a loss. When it was all still new, while the boy seemed harmless, he could shake his hand as a man of his own size (Ramos was short, too), but once he sensed just how serious things might be, he straight-out refused to see him. In the year that followed, they found signs of colon cancer. He bounced back from the surgery, more or less, but six months later he was again on the operating table since it had spread to the lungs. The second go-around, which was completely unnecessary according to the other doctors, was his downfall. The man who came out of the hospital after three weeks of recovery was a shadow of himself. Sickly legs holding up a body swollen beyond logic. He moved listlessly, his body bent to the right, his head bobbing, swaying balefully. Serge and I brought him home, cheering him on in the car, cheering him on in the elevator, cheering him on in the doorway of his house as if this threshold signaled a return to the good life. My mother and Nana shouted at the sight of this corpse, "Well, he doesn't look that bad! We'll get you freshened up in no time!" They cheered him on to the bedroom, where everything was ready—fresh pajamas, neat bed, a bouquet of flowers, cushions in place. And he, like a puppet borne by all these cheers, let himself be undressed, tucked in bed, stroked on his hands and forehead without a single word. Once he was lying under the sheets, Zora Zenaker, the housekeeper who'd been coming for years to tidy up, showed up in the doorway. Upon witnessing the scrawny, yellowish man, she'd burst out, "Oh, Monsieur Popper!" and he'd turned and pled with his crustacean arms, "Oh, my dear Zora!" She went up to the bed and they started sobbing in each other's arms: "My sweet Zora, you're the only one who can understand!"

Two months later, my father died. And with his body died the one opposing force to Ramos Ochoa. Illness had snuffed all inclination to conflict. Nana didn't speak of Ramos Ochoa anymore. And should Ramos still be lurking in the shadows, my father wouldn't be one to know. Such that, upon his death, the exiled lover who had meanwhile landed a job at Unilever was able to stride through the wide doorway of mourning and roll out the wedding carpet to no protest.

Had my father been right? Could he have, within that savage posture, been possessed of intuition and clairvoyance? And should Nana's shift in character be blamed on Ramos alone? I'm being a bit essentialist there. Spouses do interact; the transmutations that result are as unpredictable as are the faces of their progeny.

∽

At Kraków Airport, as I wait at the Hertz counter, Serge gets an email from the Walser House chef.

"Well, look at that! Wonderful!" he shouts. "Nana, Nana! I've got great news, great news. Listen, darling, Victor will be at the Walser this summer!"

"They're taking him?"

"See? Your old brother's still good for something."

"You should call Victor!"

"He knows. The chef emailed Victor and cc'ed me."

"That's just fantastic! He's going to learn more than he ever did. You know those are high international standards! He'll come back a new man. With his CV that'll be the cherry on top, I just know it."

Nana kisses him. "Thank you, my wonderful brother."

"It'll be twenty-five degrees at Auschwitz!" Joséphine reads off her phone. "Absolutely out of season for the start of April."

"I didn't pack for that . . ." Nana says.

"Microplastics are contaminating everything," Joséphine goes on. "There's a new study from the University of Newcastle saying that an average person ingests up to five grams of plastic a week. That's as much as a credit card."

"We eat that much in two minutes when we're stressed out," I say. "And I'll do it too, if that guy keeps staring at his screen."

Serge says, "Sounds like I've got enough time to pop a Mopral."

The car's a burgundy Opel Insignia. I'm the driver. Serge in the passenger seat and the women in the back.

"Turn on the AC," Serge says.

"One second."

"To the right."

"I know how to get out of a parking lot!"

"You turned on the defroster. Where's the GPS? Uh, exit! To the left! What are you doing? That's not the right spot, you've got it the wrong way around, stick the ticket under the arrow, there! Now where's the GPS? *Menu, menu . . .*"

"Enough, nobody cares."

"Nobody ever cares. I want to set up the GPS. Why is this damn thing in English?"

"Why are you all wound up?"

"It's the heat," Joséphine says.

"The heat doesn't bother me. I won't let this weather mess me up. Get ahead of that van!"

"You wanna sit in front, Jo? There's nothing worse than your dad up front."

Serge is getting on everyone's nerves as he fiddles with the GPS.

"This thing doesn't know Auschwitz. What is it in Polish? How's it spelled?"

"O-ś-w-i-ę-c-i-m."

"Head for Katowice."

"I know how to read."

"We're freezing back here," Nana whines.

Joséphine roars, "You put it on blast!"

"We can't figure out the AC."

"Turn it all off. I'm hungry, pull over if you see a restaurant."

On the highway, Serge begins explaining the Katyn massacre to us, shouting because the windows are rolled down.

"We don't care! We can't hear you, it's too windy!"

"You didn't want the AC!"

"This has to be so difficult for you, Uncle Jean," Joséphine says. "I'll completely understand if you jump out of the window."

The empty road runs past the woods. The tall trunks tight together remind me of those forests in Russian films, Wajda's *The Birch Wood*, a tight, inscrutable mystery. All the sun touched were the treetops. I recall the swaying, sublime forests of Sobibor seen in *Shoah*. The images of Lanzmann's film articulate a mental territory, a land of leafy, impervious nature. A land I now drive through.

∽

The Hotel Imperiale is that sort of narrow four-story building found in every exurban landscape in the world. That said, few hotels are surrounded by railroad tracks leading to an extermination camp. One of them, a small disused track overrun by grass between two low walls, is right outside our room. The sight strikes us as so out of place that Serge and I go to check with the front desk.

The day is winding down. According to Nana's itinerary, we are to visit Camp I and Camp II, in that order, the next day.

Before dinner, I go for a stroll with the two girls. We walk at a snail's pace along another railroad track, then down some small roads with random houses, picturesque low buildings. Nana is moving far too slowly, her jacket over her arms, her red tourist bag tracing a diagonal across her T-shirt. On her feet are ankle boots with massive, too-high heels. Her legs have gotten thicker. Her whole body has become heftier. Where has that nimble, languid neck gone? She's a small woman dressed like she's decades younger making her way along fenced-off walls and feeling too hot. Shrunken body, shrunken soul. Ahead of us Joséphine sniffs around, dolled up with too much makeup and a wild mane of hair. She has on ankle boots too, a cowboy design with fake snakeskin that propels her onward. A tall girl with an indomitable nature tackling the empty sidewalk and on the lookout for something uncertain, watching carefully for lord knows what through the holes of the fence. I went to a wedding not too long ago. The girls were dancing. They were well-built, strong. I thought, They're made to last, to bear children, to be ground down, and to resist. I saw my friend Jean-Yves straddling a chair and looking at them, and other somewhat old friends of the father left on the tile. I could tell they were losing hope.

"What's in there?" Nana asks. But Joséphine is hurtling onward, dispersing her compressed energy from one sidewalk to the next. And when Nana presses her nose to the same cracks, to the same shrubs, she says, "There's nothing there," disheartened, calling me as witness, as if there could be something to be discovered in those silent spaces in the exurbs of Oświęcim.

∽

He's sitting outside under the awning of the restaurant at the far end of the parking lot, polishing off a croque-monsieur while talking on the phone. "Papa, we're eating in just an hour!" Joséphine yells. He gives us an obnoxious wave not to interrupt his conversation. The women go up to their room.

"We might have an in on Montrouge," Serge says as he hangs up. "I've never had such a heavy croque."

"Why are you eating a croque-monsieur before dinner?"

"I was hungry."

"You had a salad an hour ago."

"I wanted a croque. Anyway, Chicheportiche might have a connection with the investigating commissioner for City Planning."

"Is that better than the mayor?"

"The mayor depends on those guys. Procedures change every five minutes. We could get a building height exemption if the municipality isn't under a Territorial Coherence Scheme. Don't ask me what that means. A shitload of but-what-ifs gussied up as a city planning code. Chiche muddles through those things. Anyway, no news from Victor."

"Did you call him?"

"Did *you* try to call him yet? Did you get hold of him? Even once? He didn't read the letter. He doesn't care. God knows where that guy is. In those sauces of his. Those tattoos of his. He's doing himself in."

Serge looks out at the parking lot, where a car's just pulled in. Guys saddled with all their equipment stagger out. He sits up. A too-tight striped shirt hugs his belly.

"You like it at Seligmann's place?"

"Nope. And it's a bad street number: twenty-seven."

"Are you holding up all right there?"

"It's not so bad. I'm four floors up. On their own the two and the seven are fine. I just mentally separate them. Two plus seven plus four make thirteen. Lucky number."

"And what about the real-estate agent?"

"No. No, no, no. Just here and there."

"So that's a yes."

"She's got her assets . . ."

"No argument there."

"She thinks I'm still living with Valentina, of course."

"Of course."

"Want a Żywiec?"

"No thanks."

I don't dare to mention Valentina. What use would it be, anyway? It all seems to be stuck at a standstill.

"Know any Poles that aren't Jewish?" he asks.

"Lemme think."

"When I drink a Żywiec I feel closer to the Poles . . . What makes a guy Polish? He just wolfs things down. He wonders what he is. He needs the devil to exist. That's me."

∽

Auschwitz, or Oświęcim if you want to be polite, is a town with the most flowers I've ever seen in my life, ever. The lampposts are wreathed in a crinoline of flowers, every fifteen meters multihued corollas are spilling out of trays, Eskimo-shaped floral statues are strutting about on the plazas, not to mention the countless shrubs and pots. The mayor must have decided: "Flourish, flourish, my dear, your town is called Auschwitz, flourish, plant, trim, clean, embellish, repaint your walls! Make your turquoise bell tower shine, polish your synagogue, make your streets a garden!"

Stenciled on a façade is Jean-Paul II alongside the words *Antysemityzm jest grzechem przeciwko Bogu i ludzkości*. Serge translates: "Jews make for good fertilizer." In front of a health and fitness center, he apes the crooked pose of the man on the poster, a grinning bald guy with terrifying muscles. At which point we notice his shoes.

"Oh, Papa, you've got those Vieux Campeur shoes on!"

"Of course."

The day is drawing to a close. At the restaurant, we opt for dinner *al fresco*. Not without some debate: the men don't want to be shut in; the women are worried about mosquitoes. The men win this round. The Portobello Ristorante was recommended by the Hotel Imperiale as Auschwitz's best restaurant. An Italian spot without a single pasta dish and boasting of its "Polish pork mit roll." Once we've ordered a risotto, a chicken club, and some pizza—we each get a different beer so we can try them all—Joséphine tells us about her boyfriend troubles. She's in love with Ilan Galoula, but he's too quiet for her. Before our trip he informed her that he can't be happy with "such a bipolar girl." They decided to take a break. She whines about not being able to watch the rest of *The Crown*, which they had started together.

"If he watches *The Crown* without me, that means it's over," she proclaims.

"Go ahead and watch *The Crown*," Serge insists. "You can't be happy with a Tunisian guy."

"Why not?"

"Because you can't."

Joséphine lets out a laugh and then regales us with the story of Serge's shoes. We already know it, of course. But it's nice to hear again. Back when Serge was living with Carole and Joséphine, Carole and a couple of their friends, the Fouérés, made plans for a vacation in the Massif Central. All five of them had gone to get shoes from Au Vieux Campeur.

"Of course, Papa had to be seen to first," Joséphine says. "He hadn't worn hiking shoes once in his life."

"Don't be silly! I went to summer camp every summer as a kid!"

"Fine, *adult* hiking shoes, then. He tried on seven or eight pairs. The first ones were too heavy, the rest were too stiff, he didn't like their color, he had to whine about his toes touching the front, there was some friction on the sides, he was in some sort of funk, it was cutting off his circulation, he already had a blister, yadda ya."

"Yes," Serge says, "it's really important to feel comfortable in the store. They tell you that you have to break in the shoes, the leather will get softer, but no, no, no, the leather doesn't get less stiff. If it hurts in the store, it'll only be worse later. That's the truth."

"So, with every new pair, Papa was going up and down the store's little one-meter-high hill to make sure the soles were good and on. After a whole hour—the saleswoman near suicidal—he decided on those soft mountain Trekking shoes you can admire on this fine evening . . . so Papa put on the shoes he'd worn into the store and the saleswomen hanging in there by a thread went on to deal with Maman and Nicole Fouéré. All of a sudden, we hear a huge crash. The set of shelves across from us had fallen over with all its display models. Screams everywhere. And on the ground, to my eternal shame, surrounded by dozens of shoes, is Papa. To kill time, he'd decided to see how good his city slip-ons were on that little hill. He'd made his way up step by step, ever so carefully. And once he got to the top, he was so blinded by his victory that he immediately fell on his face and grabbed at every single shelf in reach on his panicked way down."

We might know the story by heart, but we still laugh every single time.

"I'm no good at waiting," Serge sighs.

He gets a kick out of hearing it, too. He likes being the hero of a clownish tale. Men like to be the hero of everything, no matter what kind of hero. Joséphine comes around and hugs him. He lets her, bewildered, blushing and stiffening a little. She says, "Oh, Papa Poppet!" He gives a dumb laugh. He doesn't know how to handle this unashamed happiness.

He immediately switches to talking about beer.

"How's the Lech?"

"Decent."

"Have a taste . . . Not bad. The Tatra's a bit flat."

"I like my Okocim," Nana says.

Serge says, "What if we ordered a bitter just to see?"

Around us are a few tables of American or Polish guys. Not a crowd. The Portobello must not be on most bus routes. We toast. Joséphine snaps a shot of the three Poppers. Nana strikes a pose in between her brothers. We look happy and old.

I say, "Whatever happened to the Fouérés?"

"They're getting on in years," Serge replies. "They have a Japanese dog now. Early on they were carting it around so it wouldn't damage its little paws."

"How cute," Jo says.

"They call themselves Papa and Maman in front of their dog. 'Maman's going to give you a scolding, Papa said not on the couch.'"

"Let them," says Nana.

"Of course."

"Live and let live."

"I'm saying exactly that."

In the middle of dinner, Serge gets a call from Victor.

"Ah, here he is! Victor! So, did you see it?"

Victor didn't see a single thing. Serge gestured to convey that to us. A happy face as he prepared to announce the good news.

"Good. It's all taken care of, my boy—you've got a spot at a five-star place this summer . . . Oh, yes! . . . Well, if you checked your email you'd know what I was talking about . . . You were telling your mother that you hadn't heard back from the chef at the Walser, I took matters into my own hands, I followed up, the man's taking you on! Now you should get a move on and write him back and say thank you. And maybe you'll think to thank me, too . . . In Poland. In Auschwitz . . . Huh? . . . Huh?!"

"He doesn't want it!" Serge mouths at us, hand covering the speaker, with a look of shock and reproach aimed specifically at Nana.

"You don't want it? . . . Use French words! Victor, use normal French words, not this gibberish! . . . Fusion fast food? What the hell is that? . . . I don't understand, I don't know what this *bao* or this other thing is, I have no idea what you're talking about . . . A 'personal project'?" He gives us a stupefied look. "What's all this? You've still got snot dripping from your nose and you're talking to me about 'personal projects'? . . . My boy, you've got your whole life to waste on personal mumbo-jumbo! . . . Because your mother insisted! . . . I go out of my way, I get you a job that will open doors for you, and you tell me you've got other plans?"

"I didn't insist," Nana says.

"Listen here, Victor, you listen to me, if you don't go and work at the Walser House this summer, you can forget about me. Don't count on me to help you with a single thing, hear me? . . . All right, fine!" He slams the phone on the table.

Nana picks it up. "Hello?"

But Victor's hung up.

"He doesn't want it," Serge says in a defeated tone. "*Bao à la périgord* . . . What's this damn fast food that's going to be the end of his father who hasn't got two pennies to rub together?"

"I didn't insist."

"You did. You absolutely insisted."

He finishes his glass. There's an uncomfortable silence.

"That idiot has killed my appetite. I bend over backward and all the while he's got a 'personal project'? You'd think he might have called to let me know—'Hey, Uncle Serge! I've got a personal project that I'm gonna try to pull off this summer.'"

"Fusion fast food isn't a bad idea," Jo says.

"Oh, so this girl knows what that is! How am I gonna look in front of the chef?"

"He took two months to reply to you," Nana ventures.

"Of course! You think he's just sitting around all day? What do you think? He's really doing us a favor, looking into this himself."

"I shouldn't have asked you to follow up. It's my fault."

"Oh, stop trying to cover for him. That boy wasn't raised properly. He's got no respect for others. Simple as that. You know how he responded? 'I'm not available anymore.' Totally calm. No 'I'm sorry,' no 'Thank you so much, Uncle, but...' No nothing. 'I'm not available anymore.' Like some government official."

"He'll apologize."

"Spare me the forced apologies."

∽

We lie outstretched, T-shirts on and legs bare, on our two twin beds, with a nightstand in between. I'm the one wielding the remote control. CNN, Bolsonaro, picket lines in Warsaw, a Polish *Dancing with the Stars*, a Polish weather report...

"Keep clicking! Why'd you stop?"

"She's a pretty gal."

A TV film, some variety shows, a soccer game...

"Łódź–Białystok, who cares!"

"I don't."

"Gimme the remote, *Rambo III*, leave it, leave it!"

"It's boring."

I turn it off.

"I want to read."

"Hey, there are panties in the minibar," Serge says.

"You trust Chicheportiche?"

"Not one bit. What are you reading?"

"Primo Levi. *The Drowned and the Saved*."

"Haven't read it."

"Me either."

We're quiet for a minute.

"Can't say we've asked many questions," Serge says.

"Nope."

"Either of us. No curiosity."

"Nope."

"We really don't care in the end."

I think about it. "Yes."

He's right. We've never thought that we ought to bother ourselves with family history. For that matter, hadn't our parents themselves imposed a tacit silence? All these old stories, who wanted them?

I say, "Maybe Papa would have appreciated our being interested."

"Maybe."

Every so often, I think about my father and a sort of tenderness comes over me. It might be that it's some sort of nostalgia for oneself and for bygone times. When I watched *Shoah*, one scene made me think of him. A rapprochement wholly apart from history and its gravity. Lanzmann questions the barber Abraham Bomba, who had to cut the hair of Jewish women and reassure them before they entered the Treblinka gas chambers. Filmed in his Tel Aviv barbershop, Bomba meticulously describes the whole process in a slow, stentorian voice. All the while he's cutting, no less meticulously, strand by strand, millimeter by millimeter, the hair of a sixtysomething man, striving for imperturbability, prisoner up to his chin of a yellow cape (Who is this client who accepted such a role? Soon enough he's the only one we're watching). When he mentions the sudden appearance of friends from his town, Bomba can't talk anymore. He goes on cutting in silence, wipes his face, his eyes ... Lanzmann tells him not to stop. Bomba replies that he can't. He says *Don't make me go on, please*. He says those words in a normal tone, I mean in terms of volume level. At that point I understand that he's been reciting and breaking up his sentences to be sure of getting through to the camera and the microphone. He doesn't trust technology. He's like our father, who'd come home with a Canon 814 Super 8 in a shoulder bag. He'd spent hours at the Maison du cinéaste amateur on rue Lafayette, but he still thought the film equipment needed the oomph that would come from his subjects moving constantly and talking as loudly as possible. Abraham Bomba's naïveté, which reminded me of my father, touched me far more than his story did.

Serge gets up to rotate the lampshade on the console table. He can't have a lampshade's vertical seam (or seal) in his field of view. Such a rift in harmony is unbearable. Wherever he might be, contortions or ridicule notwithstanding, his mind won't be at ease until he's set things right. Then he goes through his suitcase and comes back to curl up in bed with a book of Isaac Bashevis Singer stories. Each of us has brought along his sliver of Jewish history.

For a minute he stares at the ceiling, and he says, "That Victor is going nowhere."

∽

I haven't slept in the same room as him since we were teenagers. Serge sleeps in a fetal position facing the bathroom wall. Coming back from a piss, I suddenly feel an impulse to get under his bedsheets and snuggle up to him the way I did at Corvol, terrified in the loneliness of the cabin. Back then, he didn't even wake up and we turned over together like lovers. How men get old and pull apart.

The silence in the Hotel Imperiale is complete. In Primo Levi, cold comes on and on. Even in a book that purports to be a reflection and not an eyewitness account, there's cold, rain, snow. Tomorrow there will be no cold nor mud nor winter. I rue this the way every traveler rues not making a trip in ideal conditions.

∽

As expected, perfect weather. Israelis wrapped in their flags do a dance of sorts amid the buses.

In the early hours, in the crush at the clearly marked entrance to Camp I, everyone's already squabbling. "I'm not running this trip," Nana grumbles upon being scolded to get in line, "it's just as much you guys as me."

"Show the lady your itinerary!"

But everyone wants to jump the line because everyone has tickets and believes they get priority. We're put in a slightly faster-moving line (we get a meter and a half ahead). Barriers, passports, security. Most of the men are in shorts, as are the women. They're looking for their group. When we emerge from the building, other wrapped Israelis are wandering on the tree-lined strip of land. At the kiosk, Joséphine grabs two guides to the camp and we buy them. We make our way forward and come to the childishly curved *Arbeit macht frei* gate that a class is posing under and that our group is waiting to be able to photograph. Beyond it are the brick buildings of the barracks. Tall trees (when do they date from?), grass on the verge. Electric poles, barbed wire. Welcome to Auschwitz.

∽

Our first impulse is to go where it's a bit less crowded. Which is how we make right for the gas chamber. An odd low structure, sinister and a way off. Downcast, silent souls keep coming out (where did we get the impression it isn't a busy area?). Groups emerging from a back alley go in. We slip in amid them, apart from Serge, who is overwhelmed by claustrophobia. It's immediately oppressive. Hurried into a dark cavern, shoulder to shoulder with people practically in beach clothes, tank tops, bright sneakers, playsuits, floral dresses, we tiptoe our way under a low ceiling toward the gruesome space. Through the shoddy grille of an opening, in a thin ray of sunshine and dust, I see Serge outside in his black suit, going in circles around himself while watching the groups get swallowed up, pounding the dry earth with his hiking shoes. I lose sight of the girls caught up in the onrush.

We cross the gas chamber, where the walls are crosshatched by scratches that everyone photographs, we walk through the crematorium room, we peer over a rope to see the ovens, the rails, the metal carts reconstituted from original materials (I read it on the placard on the way out), and we emerge, drawn outside by the light and the trees' foliage.

Nana's face crumples as she tells Serge, "You should go in."

"I can't be in crowds."

"The fingernail scratches on the walls . . . there are no words."

Serge lights a cigarette. Joséphine comes over to us.

"The scratches on the walls were really a sight, weren't they?" Nana asks.

"Really a sight," Joséphine echoes as she snaps a few photos of the crematorium's outer walls.

I find myself wondering if they will indeed say "Really a sight," "No words," and so on every chance they get. Best not to let myself get annoyed with them just yet, I figure. We press onward within the camp's confines.

∽

The overarching idea of this expedition—I'm still trying to get to grips with it—was, to put it with all the solemnity of our time, to visit the grave of our Hungarian relatives. People we never knew, who we'd never heard talk of, whose misfortunes seemed not to have upended our mother's life. But that's our family: they died because they were Jewish, they experienced the macabre fate of a people whose heritage we carry on, and in a world besotted with the word "memory," it seems ignominious to wash one's hands of such a matter. At least that's what I understand of my niece Joséphine being so feverishly invested. I try to recall what connections she might have forged with our mother. Our mother did her best not to be a link in any chain; Joséphine with her pineapple-like hairdo seems convinced she should wish otherwise.

As we pass block 24a, before we manage to curb her docent impulses, Joséphine informs us that it was a brothel, then remarks on the label about the camp orchestra.

"Are you actually wearing falsies? Today?" I ask her.

"They're permanent," she shoots back.

I can't get enough of the trees. They're everywhere. Planted properly, laid out properly. The grass also nags at me, the long, neatly mown stretches. The huge oak at the entrance must have existed back then. How tall could it have been when the camp was running? The others, those pleasant, decorative presences, were planted. By whom? What for? It would take some serious mental effort to connect the depiction in *Todeslager* with the décor we're weaving through today. I feel the same disappointment that I do before a favorite painting read about in books.

∽

The four of us wander down the paths. Two girls in flower-print shorts walk ahead of us. Their ponytails swing with each step.

I realize that I feel closer to these girls than to those Israelis making togas out of their flag. That sort of nationalistic kitsch is just plain exasperating. We have to go back and forth with Serge to get him to go into blocks 4 and 5, which serve as the museum. A crowd. We can barely breathe, and venture ever so slowly into the halls set up in a circuit. He makes two abortive attempts.

Joséphine finds him on the front steps. "Papa, make an effort. You didn't come here just to take a walk."

"I can't be in there."

"Papa, just try."

"I know it all, I already saw it all."

"Come with me. Please."

She takes him by the hand. He allows himself to be dragged into the queue, putting up with the mob and the odors of sunscreen. Once he reaches Nana at the other end of the rope, he says, shaken, "What does she want from me? What does this girl want from me?"

SS personnel with machine guns, figures with billy clubs, dogs driving the damned underground. Hundreds of white figures are crammed tight into long undressing rooms and the gas chamber depicted in the model of Birkenau crematoria. We walk in silence (and with what thoughts?) past the braces, corsets, glasses, cups, mess kits, a deep sea of vivid seashells, suitcases, shoes ("They were wearing wedges back then," Nana remarks, in front of an ankle boot set apart from the heap), hairbrushes, toothbrushes, shoeshine cases, countless silent, personal objects that had hardly foreseen becoming museum pieces. And we stop, hard put to tell whether it could be the shift or the scale that's upsetting, before the hair filling the whole space behind the pane and that couldn't clearly be said to be hair, those last human traces beloved by scientists since they can't go to dust and that nothing had preordained should become this roiling, hemp-gray mass, this interminable nest.

∽

Serge and I sit on the edge of the stones bordering the steps of block 10. The building is closed to the public. Joséphine is about to read to us from her pamphlet that this one was for medical experiments. Serge smokes. The girls come back from the bathroom. Joséphine says that the building with the restrooms also has the Hungarian pavilion but we have to go in the other side. She says that the French exhibition is the next one over. She asks what we'd rather do: see the French exhibition or the Hungarian exhibition first? She suggests seeing the French exhibition first. But in any case, she says, we should stop at the prison beforehand, block 11, the Death Block, which is the worst block because it's the torture block and has the Death Wall, where executions took place. She tells her father that she doesn't think he can smoke in the camp, she saw it in the lobby. She says, "It's stupid, in the bathroom there's a changing table! Do folks seriously come here with babies?" She says that, in the block we're sitting next to, hundreds of women served as guinea pigs for sterilization experiments.

"In 1943," she reads out loud, "the German gynecologist Carl Clauberg..."

"Enough! Jo! You're getting on our nerves!"

"What's gotten into you? He's right, you're driving us nuts!"

"I'm trying to kick this visit up a notch."

"Don't bother."

"They're idiots," Nana says.

"Aren't you hot in that outfit, Papa dear?"

"I am, I am. But you won't see me complaining about such things at Auschwitz."

∽

"I'm having a heart attack," Serge informs me in the yard where the Death Wall looms. "There's a big heavy stone on my chest and my head's spinning."

The courtyard is packed. As soon as one group trickles out of the space, another pours in. Hordes of covered or bare heads come and go through the side door of block 11. An unending onrush. It's impossible to get into the block.

"Let's get out of here," I say.

I grab him by the shoulder and try to pull him out of the mobbed inner yard while Nana gestures for us to head into the prison. We walk briskly past the buildings, our shoulders against the red walls, the basement windows. He's actually the one walking quickly while digging through his pockets.

I say, "You can't be having a heart attack if you're moving this fast."

"My jaw's like cement, that's a sign."

"No, it isn't."

"Pins and needles all over."

"Just stop for two seconds."

"I think I'm going crazy. While I was crossing yesterday, rue Marinoni flipped over."

"What are you trying to find?"

"My Xénotran."

He pulls out the blister pack. He swallows two blue pills. He wipes his forehead with a cloth. I say, "Take off your jacket, you'll boil in that suit."

"Absolutely not."

Around us is an open space ringed with low structures. We sit down on some stone siding in a shaded corner, practically on the ground. Birds can be heard.

After some time, he says, "If I go crazy someday, shoot me dead."

"It's a promise."

"If my body goes to shit, shoot me dead. Cancer, stroke, shoot me."

"Just say the word."

"Don't hem and haw."

"You're smoking while you're having a heart attack?"

"Hush!"

In front of us is the guard booth and, perched on its roof, a spindly metal weather vane. Recollections come of those stories of interminable waits while standing in deadly night, wind, ice because morning was night. The sign says, in English, *during inclement weather*. The booth is nothing, an odd little wood hut. An Asian woman in a summer poncho and those rubber clogs with holes usually seen on beaches has pulled away from her group to pose in front of it with her selfie stick. She's put on a friendly half-smile that she dials up and down with each shot.

"This booth is nothing," I tell myself, "and same for this place where so many dried-out skeletons have ended up: nothing."

My cell phone goes off.

Nana's asking: "Where are you?"

"Somewhere."

"We're coming out of the prison. It's ghastly."

"Uh-huh."

"Graves. You'd die of suffocation. How could men do that? It's unimaginable."

"It's absolutely imaginable. And it's still happening, you know."

"Why are you being so difficult?"

"Go visit Syria or Pakistan. Where are you headed now?"

"To the French pavilion. Block 20."

"We'll meet you there."

"Where are they headed?" Serge asks.

"To the French pavilion."

"They're hysterical."

∽

Day? Night? Snow's left traces everywhere, on the ties of the railroad tracks, on the dirt embankments. It stipples the black roofing with hundreds of white dots like geometrical lace. In a darkened room of the French exhibition, projected across a wall, is this photo of the Birkenau entrance gate, a slightly reddish black-and-white twilight, taken from inside the camp amid the tracks. At sky level and from the glassed-in guard booth the space is divided by wires, electric and barbed alike. Along these somber spans can be seen, in letters as gleamingly and icily white as the slide itself:

> "*Vernichttunglager*." "You know German—what does it mean?" "*Nichts* means 'nothing, nothingness. Toward nothing, nothingness.' In other words, 'Annihilation Camp.'"
> —Charlotte Delbo, *Convoy to Auschwitz*

In a single image, the allegory of desolation hits the reader. Images overpowering reality. Reality needs interpretation to remain real.

Joséphine tries to take in the whole wall.

Serge makes a point of staying out of pace with us. We catch him in front of the computer with the names of French deportees. He didn't find anyone. No Malkovsky matches up to Sacha, the Hopts are from Lyon, Jacky's grandfather Armand Alcan isn't there.

He says, "This database is useless."

"Type 'Nathilde Pariente,'" Nana requests.

Serge steps back from the monitor and leaves.

"What's with him? Is he pissed off at me?"

"Of course not."

"He hasn't said a word to me since this morning."

"I've got someone too," Joséphine says.

It's a game. I have names to look for too, names of French Jews. I find some. But I can't be sure the names that come up are the people I know. I'm almost disappointed.

～

"Remember" is written on the sign. "Remember. Nearly seventy-five thousand Jews were deported from France, more than eleven thousand of them children." We hear an odd train sound between two rooms . . . (The designers must have thought: Let's give the visit a touch of drama with a railroad noise.) Dozens of photos of children, their names, their dates, their stories in five lines: Martha and Senta, the girls from Izieu in their nice coat with gold buttons; Bernard Edelstein 37 rue Mathieu in Saint-Ouen; Édith Jonap, Limoges boarding school; Simon Abirjel 15 rue Clavel in Paris's 19th arrondissement; Lucien, arrested in Vouvant in the Vendée . . . look at their faces, their names, their prim haircuts, notice that nothing in their stance hints at their brief existence, read their convoy number, be struck by the sentimentality, practically say like your sister that it's *unspeakable*, ask forgiveness of the little ghosts (for the rest of humanity) and feel better for three minutes, but come back out in the sunlight, to the car, and what will you remember? If you even remember?

∼

Outside, a call from Paulette. Maurice's been revived. Last night they celebrated the evening nurse's birthday.

"We celebrated Iolanda's thirtieth," Paulette says. "She's his favorite, you know. Maddie was there and the building staff came up. Believe it or not, Maurice had his beloved champagne, he didn't want his salmon sandwich but he liked his bite of stuffed cabbage, he doesn't like salmon anymore, 'Oh do you not like salmon anymore, Maurice?' He said no, his tastes have changed. I'll hand you over. You'll see, his French's not back to what it was but slow and steady does the trick. I'll hand you over now, Jean! *Jean!*" She's yelling.

"Hello?"

"Maurice?" I say (or shout).

"Is that you?"

"Yes, it's me, Maurice."

"Ah, good!" Some violent spitting sounds. "The Gypsies that came back to the ulipol, do you remember them?"

"The *ulipol*?"

"The uli . . . ulibolshoi, yes . . . be, because . . ." Some words that must be Russian. "Do you remember them?"

"Yes, I remember them."

"Good. Because I don't think I'll see my soul."

"No."

"Ha ha ha."

"Ha ha ha."

"He's doing better, isn't he?" says Paulette, who's taken the phone.

"I think so."

"He wants to drive again, that's a good sign."

"Not for everyone it is."

"And, you know, he's not that comfortable on the phone, we'll have to get his hearing aids checked, I don't think they're well-suited for that, there's a loose wire . . ." I hear a groan. "Yes, Maurice, it's loose! But I don't care about your hearing!"

"And he's talking in Russian a bit."

"Yes. He's talking in Russian. That's his mother tongue, naturally."

"So it is."

In the driver's seat, Maurice had always been a public menace. One day I told him, "Serge told me he's been feeling a bit afraid in the car with you these days."

"Really? With me?"

"Yes, with you."

"Okay . . ."

"He told me you ran a couple of lights that might not have needed running."

"I've been doing that all my life."

∞

Serge's waiting for me. "All these kids, what a pain in the ass," he says, "that's why Europe's going down the drain. They've killed the living soul of Europe. The few of us Jews left aren't good for bupkis. Look at those numbskulls we've got now."

"Maurice's on the up-and-up, you should go see him."

"Sure, sure. Yeah. Why haven't I done it yet? Oh right, I'm disgusting."

"He's always asking about you."

"No excuses. Well, when we get back, I'll go over."

I drag him to the upper level of block 18, where, in an especially dimly lit setup, we find the Hungarian exhibition. There's almost nobody there. A couple at the back, two or three folks walking around, Nana and Jo bent over plexiglass desks filled with railroad gravel on which the history of Hungary's Jews can be read. Granitoid heaps and transparent stones blanket the ground. Unruly assemblages of slides are projected on the walls in oval vignettes. In the middle of this mausoleum: a notional wagon of tinted plexiglass. Under the glass pane supporting it: railroad tracks and some ballast made of clear crystals. Serge heads straight for one of the few uncovered windows adjoining the bastard Otto Moll projected as a medallion. I do a quick lap. There's Clauberg, the gynecologist. There's Mengele and the Hungarian dwarfs. And that bitch Maria Mandl, the SS supervisor. Oh, denizens of the Budapest ghetto! Those women in single file with their hands up. Come and see: an aunt, a cousin? Our mother? I inspect the faces. I could practically make out the family's features. I look for Zita, too. Zita Feifer née Roth, whose whole family died in the camps and who we'd abandoned after our mother's death. And even in the welter of chaotic images, those same funereal processions down the railroad tracks. A hunched-over woman walks toward a crematorium in a headscarf and enormous coat, notwithstanding the sunshine and thin rain boots. I stare at her a long while. She looks like Nanny Miro, who watched us when we were little. A woman about whom we knew nothing at the time except that she was from the Jura, a word that didn't mean much to us either, and who we called "Nanny" like the British. A woman whose life had not been gentle, whose body was now bloated; I can still feel that coat's heft between my fingers.

Joséphine and Nana are moving along from one desk to the next like good schoolchildren.

"You can read all of that at leisure in Paris," I say.

"Daddy, what are you looking at?"

"The tree."

"Are you sick of the exhibition?"

"Completely."

"You could take some interest, you know," says Nana.

"But why?"

"Oh, don't be like that. You're getting on my nerves."

"Look at these pictures, Papa."

Joséphine has taken his arm and dragged him to the two huge panels at the end of the space. A young woman from

Budapest is posing, pleasingly plump, in a beach-patterned bikini with her little girl and her husband. On the other panel, she's barely standing, bracing herself on a bed frame. She's unrecognizable, naked, nothing but skin and bones; patches of hair are missing. The caption explains that she's come out of Bergen-Belsen and her name is Margit Schwartz. Between the two photos, one year has elapsed. The first is somewhat unreal. The swimmers' arrangement in the background, the shape-shifting palm trees' branches are like a painted backdrop. Serge stays in front of those two images for a while. What is he thinking about? He has a knack for being exhausting; he's also an expert at silence. In that suit of his, he strikes me as elegant. He's dressed to the nines. Even his Vieux Campeur shoes look nice.

I wonder who donated these photos to the museum. Margit Schwartz herself? I know she and her daughter survived, because I checked. What about the husband in a dark swimsuit? There's no information about him.

∼

Back to wandering outside down the camp's paths.

Remember. But why? So as not to do it again? But it will be done again. Knowledge that isn't closely connected to oneself is useless. One can't expect anything of memory. This fixation on memory is a sham. When Macron was making his so-called *itinérance mémorielle*, a cab driver summed it up for me: "Last night, I saw the report from Verdun. They told them all there's fifteen thousand dead beneath your feet, guts out in the air! Tourists in raptures. They're there with their kids: Grandpa fought for you. And the kids say: 'For me? But how does he know me?'"

These omnipresent rows of poplars! They must look appropriately bare in winter. The barracks are tidy, well-maintained. It's a museum. A stretch of limbo revamped for modern-day visitors. A noble gesture that makes things opaque.

∼

"The gas chambers have been defunct for seventy-five years now," Joséphine says. "Since November '44."

"Can we get just two minutes to eat?"

All the outside tables under the Hotel Imperiale's awning are taken. A boisterous horde of Polish and American customers. A girl brings us coffee. We'd asked for toothpicks; there aren't any. Nana comes out with a handful of dry cookies instead.

"Sometimes I dream about filling out my teeth," Serge says.

"What do you mean?"

"Getting myself a set of cipollino marble dentures. A flat thing, no gaps. I'm gonna kill the guy yelling behind me."

"Papa, calm down."

"I'm getting old enough that I can do with a bit of smiting here and there. With one of those tridents. Or a dagger like the blades on those Lebel bayonets."

"How in heaven is it so hot?" Nana wonders. "Is it global warming? The Hungarian exhibition was a huge disappointment."

"What were you expecting?"

"You know the barbed wire is fake. It gets replaced every ten years to mimic the Nazi model..."

"Give that guidebook here, Joséphine."

"They're made that dark on purpose... The columns are the original ones but they rust..."

"Jo!"

"She's got years of philistinism to make up for," Serge says.

"So sweet."

"But now she knows how to say Auschwitz."

"Auschwitz."

"Very good. Now: Majdanek, Sobibor..."

"Majdanek, Sobibor."

"Chełmno..."

"I'll take a class on Judaism."

"That, too."

"No, no, you've got it! Well done, my girl."

"*Looking for a dentist*..." I whisper in English in his ear.

Serge cracks up.

"What is it?" Nana asks. "What?"

"Don't overdo it on the cookies, Papa."

"Get these away from me. I'm on a diet and she brings me cookies!"

Nana laughs. "You're on a diet? Ha ha ha."

"Hey, who's bankrolling Victor's fast food? You?" Serge asks.

"I don't see how that's happening."

"Our dear Ramos has a nice little nest egg, doesn't he? Under one of his floorboards?"

I laugh and nod.

"Ramos works harder than any of us at this table," Nana cuts in. Her tone is icy.

"I'll bet he does!"

"Why are you laughing?"

"Oh sure, he works hard. Keeping track of all those government benefits and short-term contracts and worker's comp payments, it's a full-time job . . ."

"Which takes some real skill!" I add.

Serge mimes a little juggling act.

"Those short-term contract bonuses are going down!"

He falls back and collects himself. "Ha ha ha!"

"Unless that nest egg just goes to paying off the Torre dos Moreno shack?"

"Don't you call it a shack!" Nana squeals.

We burst out laughing.

"A shack made of three boards on some sand with fish bones everywhere!" Serge says.

"Ha ha ha!"

"Okay, Papa, stop. Don't be stupid."

Only Nana isn't laughing.

"Teach some life lessons, Serge, why don't you. Who better than you . . ."

"I'm the last one who should be teaching life lessons. But I'll gladly take a few apologies."

"You were saying last night, save the apologies."

"I mean actual apologies. That boy of yours needs to learn a few things."

"Pass those cookies back to your father, Jo," I say.

"Let's go to Birkenau," Joséphine says.

Nana's walled herself off.

"You go on ahead without me."

Marion calls. I talk on the phone while walking around the Hotel Imperiale's parking lot where the guests' cars are parked. The other section had been empty the night before; now it has a dozen buses. We're each in our own corner, our little quartet dispersed across this soulless, gray ground, notwithstanding the sun, under which stiff oncomers wearing straw hats and caps while dragging bags and suitcases wander.

Marion wants me to come along to Luc's school event. I don't like those events. Packed spaces, unbearable conviviality. I went to one back in kindergarten. Lined up at the front of the stage and trussed up in red crepe-paper outfits, the children sang a counting rhyme. Luc capped off the line with his eyes staring into the void while the others mimed the words with their hands. In fits and starts, as if struggling to be one with the whole, he picked up a word. He could be heard saying, out of time, and out of tune, "through the window" or even "open me." He also sometimes made rabbit ears or a house roof when the others were doing deer antlers. His eagerness moved me deeply. Marion laughed. I knew it wasn't a genuine laugh, but laughter was the most convenient thing. I myself had to hold back from grabbing the kid and dragging him out of the room and far from all this monkey business.

"When's the event?"

"We've got time," Marion says, "it's in June. This is just a heads-up."

I ask what he was going to do. She doesn't know. I say I'll come. And then, driven by an urge to torment myself, I ask, "Why don't you take the Argentine guy?"

"He isn't Argentine," she says, then adds, "He gets on my nerves."

"He's annoying?"

"We're not getting into that over the phone. How's Auschwitz?"

"Why does he get on your nerves?"

"It doesn't matter. Where are you?"

"In a parking lot."

"How is it all?"

"Fine, fine."

He annoys her!

I get into the driver's seat of the Opel and honk at the other family members.

༄

"Birkenau means 'birch grove,'" says Joséphine in the car as we pull out of the lot. Nobody speaks after that. No signs direct us to Camp II. I follow the railroad tracks. I turn off the main road and head down half-abandoned paths where we glimpse railroad pylons beyond the swamplands. We turn around. There isn't a living soul. Serge puts up no protest, his listless body bouncing with all the jolts and bumps, Nana sulks with her nose against the window, her eyes on the landscape.

Joséphine is the only one who cares about our meandering. "They wouldn't have this sort of road to get to Birkenau!"

I do a U-turn. We cross a more wooded area and come to a meadow.

On the wholly unused railroad tracks are two seemingly lost train cars. Two connected wood-and-iron train cars, what had been called cattle cars, with barred doors, too tall to get down from normally. Cars from another time, far too modest for the present-day landscape, so fragile atop their wheels that look like they've come from old Swiss toys. I stop the car. Joséphine and I get out, followed by Nana. We're as alone as this poor coupler. We walk down the tracks; there are a few candles in a row and some commemorative plaques. On the bed of dark stones, a white pebble on which someone has written *Past or Future?* in Sharpie. The sky is overcast in spots, darkening as though before a storm.

"Come here, Papa," Joséphine shouts.

We hear a freight train going past behind the trees. A sound from another era in the fuzzy silence of the countryside. But which other era? I wonder. The mind will concoct fanciful connections. Back when this place served as a platform, there wasn't any silence, only chaos and a woebegone hubbub. Places are deceitful. Just like things.

"Papa, come see! It's the *Judenrampe*!"

Right in front of us are houses fronting the road. One has a red roof and ocher walls. In its huge yard is a welter of miniature arrangements and attractions. Portico, swing, slide, shed, flowers, Christmas-sized pine trees, wooden windmills, painted pinwheels stuck to the perimeter. A teensy Neverland for all to see and enjoy, and with a harmless fence giving the presumably present children a perfect view of the railroad tracks, the two train cars stranded in the future, like a garland as backdrop.

"Get out of the car, Papa, it's the *Judenrampe*!"

"Leave me be."

"Five hundred thousand deportees came here!"

"I don't care."

"This is the worst place in the world, Papa!"

"Bugs are attacking me."

"Come on, then!"

"No."

"I want you to see things with me."

"I'm staying in the car."

"Leave him be! If he wants to stay in the car, let him," Nana says. "I don't know why you wanted to drag your father along. He's ruining the day for us; he's been a wet blanket on this trip. It's incredible that we're alone. Why don't people come here?"

"It's for the best," I say.

"Yes, but."

Who's living in this ocher house? Why didn't they have a hedge or plant a few trees to shield it?

Joséphine's opened the car door and is trying to pull her father out. She yanks on him, bracing herself. He resists. She's strong. He has to fight to stay put. He bursts out laughing.

"Papa, why are you doing this?!" she shrieks. She groans, bent double, her pineapple hairdo masking her face. Unable to get him out, she lets go. Nana rushes over. Joséphine is red and puffy-faced. She's sobbing as she says, "I hate him! I hate you!" Serge slams the car door and locks himself in. Nana tries to pull Joséphine into her arms. Joséphine shakes herself free and dashes off, sniffling, toward the ruined walls (which turn out to be the remnants of a potato storehouse).

"You really can be an idiot!" Nana says, hitting the Opel's window.

I go back and sit in the driver's seat. Serge's smoking. I say, "That's the *Judenrampe*."

"What's the *Judenrampe*? I've had it up to here with this *Judenrampe*."

"That's where the Jews came, for the most part."

"Okay. I see it. I see all of it from the car."

"I'm just telling you what it is."

"I've had it with both of them pigging out on misery."

"You could be kinder with Jo."

"She's obsessed. Eyebrow school yesterday, the extermination of Jews today. And everyone's got to go along with her fixations. And aside from that she doesn't show any sign of life unless she wants money or an apartment."

"Enough."

"That little Tunisian guy, Ilan Galoula, he chickened out. And I can see why."

"How's the apartment stuff coming along?"

"It isn't. I'm broke and there's no way I can ask Valentina to remain a guarantor now."

In the distance, Nana's on the phone. She's walking up and down along the tracks. When I take in the scene through the Opel's window, it strikes me as insignificant and featureless. And yet, when we get back from this trip and I remember this, this image is the one that will overshadow all the others. My sister with her too-heavy boots and her red messenger bag across her chest, walking with her head down and her shoulders stiff, up and down the tracks in front of the two lost train cars. I'll see the two hooks at each end of the coupler, the huge wheels like cartwheels. The trees in the background, the gravel, the empty road. When I reread books, at the word *Judenrampe* I'll see Nana on the phone pacing back and forth by herself in front of the old wooden train cars with their wrought-iron bars.

"Are we staying here for a thousand years?" Serge asks. "What lunatic built this hovel?"

I go out to get Joséphine. She's on the phone as well. She follows me, crabby. She snaps pictures of the ruin (at this point she thinks it's an old fortification for Camp II). She snaps pictures (for the fiftieth time) of the train cars, she snaps pictures of the ocher house. She's been snapping pictures nonstop since this morning.

"What are you going to do with all these pictures?"

She shrugs.

～

The Birkenau camp is huge. Dizzyingly huge. Past the gate we enter a realm devoted to death. The inevitability of this label is undeniable. That itself is dizzying. No pretenses. The train tracks go straight toward death. All paths, sooner or later, lead there. At Birkenau, the industrial project of annihilation is evident. All human activity and the spaces to shelter them are in service of death.

At Birkenau there is nothing to do but walk. We approach the hills. Rays of sunlight still come down. On the ramp, a man plays at throwing a child up in the air.

Every so often a security guard comes through on a Segway. Practically a supersonic roly-poly in a light-blue short-sleeve shirt who goes through a barbed-wire door and disappears behind a hut.

We walk down the railroad tracks. The tracks built to receive Hungarian Jews. No sooner were they out of the train than they were filing down the same path straight to the gas chamber. I try to see what they saw. But nothing can be seen. Not the endless expanse of grass. Not the rubble. Not the ghostly, tidy sheds.

A lawnmower can be heard in the distance. A wind presaging stormy weather brings the scent of mountains.

We walk on a path belonging to no particular time. And we ourselves have no idea what has led us there. I see my brother's body. Sunday best and gray hair. He strikes me as less solid. Maybe even stumbling a bit.

He's like our father going back up rue Méchain wearing a jacket with overstuffed shoulders and billowing tails. I took him to Cochin Hospital just two months before he died. A stupid, pointless meeting to get a prostate exam from a big-shot buddy of a boss at Motul. My father was dressed up to make a good impression. The building was deserted because Mitterrand had just had an operation there. On the way out, we were mobbed, microphones out, by a pack of reporters cooling their heels. "He's doing well," my father said calmly before the first question had come, "the 'Patient' is doing well. Good evening to you, sirs!" And on the strength of his status as a special visitor, he strode off with pleasant condescension. He went back up rue Méchain, drowning in the too-big suit, delighted that his voice had rung so loud, delighted to have cheated death and come off as a close acquaintance of the president. I couldn't say that he was limping, but that his body, similarly, had been tilting to the side with each step as if weighed down by an invisible burden.

I see Nana on her own up ahead, the red messenger bag across her back. I'm overcome by fondness for this little woman who's weathered the years. I could just dash over, surprise her, kiss her on the neck. I see my brother and sister and me on this road lined by chimneys and dead stones and I wonder what fate landed all three of us in the same nest, not to mention the same life. Behind us Joséphine indulges her photo obsession.

What if I married Marion, I think. Why leave the privilege of a proper upbringing to the Ochoas? How old is she? Forty. She could still have another kid. I'll get a dog for Luc. A short-haired mongrel. Luc will play around with his dog and his brother. I'll be welcomed home by shrieks of joy and barking, I'll toss my jacket on a chair piled up with clothes.

We walk down the path leading nowhere. We'll see the ruin, a hideous flattened ruin in fragrant springtime. There are no ghosts beside us. People meander up ahead. As there's no right pace here, we meander like them. Serge stops to light a cigarette. He hunches to protect himself from the wind.

Here's the ruin. The destroyed remnants of gas chambers and crematoria. Caved-in buildings likely covered in weed killer. Right by them is the monument to the victims: paving stones with larger stone blocks on top engraved in several languages. Serge hands me his phone. A message from Victor.

Uncle Serge, I read the chef's email. I got it yesterday but everyone knows I'm not glued to my phone esp. since I get like 1 email a month. I have to ask: did you read it? Really read it? I don't think you did. You should. The chef's offering me a two-week stage like I'm an apprentice, but I'm applying for a full season in a team as a COOK. (So you know: the last place I worked in is Chez Treuf, where I really made an impression, I went from commis au froid to chef de partie aux cuissons in just four months.) Meaning that I'm aiming for demi-chef de partie at the very least. So, I don't feel any regret in turning down this offer. Like I said on the phone, my email never received an answer; in the meantime, other opportunities have come up. I never asked you to get back in touch with the chef. I need you to understand that I live my life apart from my mother and I wasn't aware that she had asked you to do so. You are my uncle. But given our relationship over the past few years, I'm more inclined to say that you are the brother of my mother. It's saddened me that you've shown so little interest in me and for so long. I am asking you to stop speaking to me in this condescending, authoritarian tone for no good reason. You are not my father, nor my boss, nor a "sensei" of some other sort. I owe you nothing. Your threat will not and does not have any hold over me. I am grateful to you for having tried to secure me a position in this Swiss hotel, but I don't need your help in general. I just need a family. Victor.

"What a little shit," Serge says.

"He's young."

"What a little shit."

"He'll get over it."

"That tone of his. That arrogance. A prick right out of school."

"Ramos takes that tone."

"'I need a family'! Who needs a family? It disgusts me."

"That's his father, too."

"What the hell are we doing here? Let's get a move on, Jean. All these plaques talking to humanity? All these ugly stones!"

I pull him in tight. His head against mine as he whispers, "I hate it all."

How nice the light is. Behind us is some underbrush. Some pinkish trails amid the tall trees. They run the length of the fencing and the peaceable watchtowers. In Svetlana Alexievich's oral history of Chernobyl, above the deserted area birds cavort and "the sky is blue as blue."

Nana and Jo join us. I say, "We've seen our fair share, haven't we? Shall we head out?"

"Oh no," Joséphine says. "We have to see the Sauna!"

"What's the Sauna?" Serge asks.

"It's the disinfection and processing building."

"Go without me."

Nana turns crimson.

"You didn't want to go into the gas chamber, you didn't want to see the *Judenrampe*, you made a point of boycotting the Hungarian exhibition, and now the Sauna! Would it kill you, Serge, if just once in your life you could put your ego aside and go along with a group, just for a single day, to make your daughter happy!"

I give her a gentle pat on the shoulder, but that only makes matters worse.

"You could just be quiet and look. But no, you have to make a spectacle of yourself. What are you trying to prove? That you've seen it all already? That you're not a tourist? We know you're not happy to be here. You don't have to broadcast it every second. I'm sorry; I took a plane to Kraków to see with my own eyes the places where thousands of people died horribly, people in our family, people we could have known personally. Serge Popper has learned the lessons of these horrors, that's great, congratulations, but I haven't, and neither has your daughter. And who knows about Jean, he's your toady. Your toady!"

"What lessons? There's no lesson to learn from this," Serge says.

"Keep being insufferable, then."

"Go! Go on to the Sauna!"

"Stop it, Papa! She's right, you're being negative and mean!"

"I mean it, go now! Be so good as to have a look at the Sauna. I'm not standing in anyone's way."

"He's being ridiculous. Come on, Jo," Nana says.

"Okay."

"Go, Jo. Go explore the camp with your aunt. And Victor couldn't care less what we're doing here."

"What's Victor got to do with anything?"

"He just texted me."

"Did he?"

"Go to the Sauna."

"Stop it with the Sauna. What did he say?"

"There are words I don't understand, but apparently I'm not his uncle and I can go to hell."

"Show me."

"And apparently he's an experienced chef! Just look and see!"

"He's a chef."

"Of course."

Nana grabs his jacket, rummages in its pockets, and pulls out the phone. Joséphine calmly keys in her father's code. They read Victor's message together. At the end, Jo says, "That's funny of Victor."

"A two-week stage!" Nana shrieks. "How did you expect him to be happy about that?"

"You don't think it's odd that he sent me that while I'm at Auschwitz?"

"What's that got to do with anything?"

"You tell me!"

"We're not under Hitler's thumb. You're not in striped pajamas."

"Plenty of folks would kill for a two-week stage at the Walser."

"Not when you've got an Émile Poillot diploma! And not when you're looking for a full season's paid work!"

"The chef didn't even know Émile Poillot."

"He's a rube! Everyone knows Émile Poillot! Did you read the email? You didn't read it!"

"What do I know about cuisine! I put the two of them in touch, it's on them to figure things out. It's not my fault if Victor Ochoa is the only kid on earth who doesn't check his phone."

"You yelled at him like he'd turned down the job of the century!"

"Yelled! Is this boy made of sugar or something?"

"You reamed him out over the phone. You humiliated him."

"About time someone talked to him, mano a mano! He's never had a proper education. A pathetic excuse for a father and you've made a faggot of him!"

"Papa, you didn't just say that!"

"What?" He took a few steps with his arms limp. "They never should have abolished the military service."

"Just wait two seconds, he'll tell you that he's ended up staff sergeant and his men love him," Joséphine says.

"That's the absolute truth."

"Can we just agree on one thing?" Nana cuts in, on the verge of tears. "That you stop it, and same goes for you, Jean, now and for all time, with badmouthing Ramos! I don't want to hear another word out of either of you about Ramos! I don't even want to hear his name out of your mouths, ever again!"

Joséphine hugs her tight and looks at us angrily.

"You have a point," I say. "It's a promise."

I already know I won't be keeping that promise.

To take the edge off, I add, "Let's see the woods. Is the Sauna that way?"

I clap Serge's back to get him to come along. We set off in silence. I recognize the woods. The men had stood talking, the women and children had sat at the foot of the trees. In this birch grove, the Hungarian Jews had awaited their turn in the gas chamber. They had known nothing of their imminent fate. We saw the photos this morning. In one, a tiny child had been offering a bigger one a dandelion.

We're alone. The sun is sporadic through the leaves. Nana sways in her high boots. Suddenly she turns around and says to Serge, lagging a few meters behind, "Where's the success in your life? I don't see it."

He stops, takes a drag on his cigarette, and says, "I don't either."

"You go around acting all condescending, you act like you're doing us a favor, you spend your time judging other people's lives as if yours was something to be proud of."

"No I don't!"

"The way you talked about the Fouérés last night. You always have to be snickering, getting a laugh in. They pull their dog around in a cart, they call themselves Papa and Maman! If they want to call themselves that, so be it! It's not as pathetic as looking around for people's weaknesses. What's so special about your life? You've spent it looking for trouble. You're sixty, you don't have a house anymore, your affairs are a mess, your property manager's ripping you off . . ."

"He's putting me up."

"Oh, how nice. I don't get why you're being so high-and-mighty. Monsieur Serge Popper does something for someone once in his life, and we have to clap for him for ten years after? You're completely out of your mind, you sad sack. I spend my days dealing with people in actual precarity, who are on the absolute brink, some of their kids have never seen the sea or the mountains, and I can tell you it's a real luxury to go looking for nits to pick yourself. Don't you give me that look! Whenever

I talk about my work I have to hold back because I don't want your stupid snickering. Like it or not, I'm happy helping other people, I'm proud to be supportive, to be part of a thoughtful society, I think it doesn't make any sense to live for oneself alone. One day you'll end up all alone in a hole, Serge. Because you've lost an incredible woman who kept you from going under. I don't understand how you managed to lose Valentina!"

"Mind your own business."

"Well, you make it your own business when you badmouth Ramos, when you and your ass-kissing brother imply that he doesn't do anything, that he's lying to the unemployment office, when you insist that he's not a good father when there's nobody more thoughtful, more devoted to his children than Ramos . . ."

"The Nazis were also devoted to their children. Stangl was a good father, Goebbels was a good father, I can give you a whole list of good fathers who loved their families. Children are the easiest thing to be devoted to. That doesn't mean anything. And likewise for families."

"Very nice for Jo to hear that."

Joséphine shrugs. She's busy snapping pictures, tree trunks in the foreground, of the ruins of Crematorium III.

"I don't know what you can bring yourself to care about," Nana says. "Honestly, I feel like it's nothing. That's pathetic. Give me a cig."

"Why do you want one, Nana?" Joséphine asks.

"Because I'm smoking today!"

And now she's smoking with her lips stuck out. And now it's raining. The pinkish trails disappear all of a sudden and we hear a distant thunderclap. "Shit!" Nana yells. "How far are we from the Sauna, Jo?"

They start running in the underbrush. We hurry in their wake. The rain coming down is unreal. It's a deafening, cruel, heavy rain. It's all around us, coming from the sky, the trees, and maybe elsewhere, it hits us with a vengeance, we rush forward blindly through its disorienting racket, branches scratching, we can't keep our eyes open. Our feet sink down, the earth is already muddy. Mud! There's that famous mud, the vile sludge mentioned in books. It sucks in bodies, it's hungry, what an experience to take in its rising scent, hear its plop and splatter, and how disgusted, how ashamed I am by this bizarre feeling. The girls are running, stumbling through the tree trunks; we can pick out their muffled yelps.

∽

At the edge of the forest is a marshy expanse, at the end of which an utterly desolate and nondescript building weathers the storm. We hurtle, sodden, toward its courtyard, where a station wagon is parked. Everything's deserted: the doors are shut and through the locked windows empty hallways can be seen. Is this the Sauna? This building curled in on itself, the *Zentralsauna*, the antechamber of hell of which the escapees speak?

Joséphine hammers at the doors and yells, "Is anyone inside?" The torrent literally slaps us. All around are huge puddles, practically ponds, and rectangles of turf surrounded by stones and dying reeds. As we inch along the brick walls in hopes of finding a way inside, I think back to Margot's philosophy professor, that extravagant Cerezo that the whole class had made fun of. Monsieur Cerezo in his huge parka who came back each year to tread the moors of the dead like a madman of tragedy. He's got it right, I think. The only way we should cry for the camp's dead is fanatically. I feel a retroactive pang for this man and his unceasing yet doomed attempts to convey this.

A bit farther off, on the other side, someone's come out of a doorway and is doing his best to open an umbrella undone by the tornado. We rush over to get into the Sauna.

∽

Dreadful return.

In the evening, driving toward Kraków, we pass a small biplane in a field.

"An Antonov," Serge says weakly.

"That's right!"

"An Antonov 2. The Jeep of the tundra."

His sole words during the drive. The landscape is disfigured by billboards.

"You've gotten sunburnt, Papa. You're bright red."

"Rub some aloe on him," I say.

Joséphine starts humming strangely.

"Did you know that beards protect against the sun?"

"Interesting."

"You're real fun in this car."

She turns back to her phone.

Our route follows the railroad tracks. Modern-day tracks, perhaps, on a small hill abutting the road. Do we pay attention to the tracks under normal circumstances?

In the middle of total silence Joséphine says, "The ice caps are melting seven times faster than twenty years ago."

"We're headed for disaster," Nana says.

"Arctic warming will set off a baby boom of spiders."

"Enough with your phone."

"It's not the phone, it's the world. I'll catch my death with this wet hair. Turn on the heat, Uncle Jean. And just so you know, rain's full of microplastics too."

The Fouérés have adopted a dog. No surprise there. They're the sort of couple who don't settle until their old age. After years of ups and downs, they end up happy together: taking trips, adopting dogs, sometimes buying up a farmstead somewhere. For all her life Nicole's been striving for someone other than Jean-Louise; when they weren't bickering, the Fouérés were tearing each other to pieces with scathing *bons mots*. But at a certain point, they saw death giving them a little wink and they lay down their arms. Life can be a lonely thing so long as there's a future.

I know plenty of folks whose shared interests have swept existential hopes under the rug. I've actually felt jealous at times of this grim victory.

The deportees who returned in hats and heavy furs for lord knows what memorial service have now joined those already dead. That's a particular variety of old people, lost amid their outsize coats, bundled up in cold-weather clothing that make them look like they have no neck, people from another era never to be seen again. Without them, this place wouldn't exist anymore. What's the use of the struts, the lawn mower, the well-maintained brickwork, the tiles, the wood beams after them? When they die, so do a century and a continent.

Intermarket, Auto Komis, Brico. It doesn't feel like a different country. On both sides of the highway, day lingers on a few valleys. I suddenly feel overcome by nostalgia for Miami (where I've never been). A balcony, let's say the fourteenth floor, in the fifties. Night. Warm weather, the smell of gas and marsh plants. The skyscrapers' light visible through the railing. Me sitting in a plastic chair, life going by, the ocean, the sounds of traffic. Me as an old man, with all the melancholy of a plastic armchair, of a banana tree in its tiny pot.

Where'd all that come from?

∾

Zita's survived three husbands and buried a son. Feifer was the last name of her third husband, her great love. When she was young, she was a dead ringer for Gloria Swanson. Same lips, same long pinched nose, same boyish haircut. She smoked with a cigarette holder and laughed with lipstick traces on her teeth. Our mother used to say: "She likes *men*," and Father—oh, how discreetly!—would nod approvingly. Her son died in the Swiss Alps while trying to grab a raspberry at the edge of a ravine. What Zita kept were her Hungarian accent and her predilection for using the wrong gender for particular nouns: the masculine for "a spoonful," the feminine for "a chignon." She powdered her face with Poudre de riz de Java (the name was on the lime-green tin), which smelled so tantalizing.

Maurice was her lover during her second husband, an art dealer. When the dealer was away, she'd welcome Maurice into her place with a positively medieval array of candles, including those in two seven-armed candelabras. She invited him in American-style with a gin rickey and sat like a lewd gamine on a low chair while Maurice sipped his cocktail and eyed her crotch. We learned all this from Maurice, who likely embellished a bit, but our mother, who heard everything from Zita, confirmed the broad brushstrokes. After some time, Zita took the gaucho whip from the pampa down off the wall, begging Maurice, "Whip me!" Sometimes she put the Swiss axe in his hands and knelt, stretching her neck toward the blade: "Slaughter your dove! Drink my blood, Moritz!" They had a great time together. Other days, the mood was more difficult. Maurice had a weakness for her teeth. "Bite me, little beaver," he'd say, as she furrowed her muzzle, stuck out her magnificent incisors, and began nipping at him.

Max Feifer put a stop to those peccadilloes. He was a furrier, kept kosher, had a scarab's chest and a heavy-lidded eye. He was a funny, proper little man, and we loved him. His hair stuck up in a plum tarboosh of sorts rounded off by white sideburns. One day, our mother told Zita, "You ought to tell Max not to use such an intense dye," and she replied, "Wait, he's dyed?!"

Max is dead now. Maurice and Zita are waiting their turn, locked up in their respective apartments. They must have forgotten each other. But, I think to myself, what existed can't not have existed.

~

In the Kraków Radisson's bathroom, we gobble teensy mint after teensy mint from a bowl on the counter where they've sat for a hundred years. I'm in a bubble bath, Serge on the toilet. Ten minutes later, his phone rings: Valentina Dell'Abbate.

"Valentina! She's calling! Hello?" He heads off into the bedroom. All I hear is the occasional murmur.

He's come back to sit on the porcelain. He unwraps another piece of candy. The trash can overflows with transparent wrappers. He sucks on the candy and stares at the bubbles with bulging eyes.

Finally, he says, "Marzio wants me to be there for his birthday."

"That's nice."

"Do you think it's Marzio or her?"

"Both of them."

"You think it's just to make her son happy? Or does she want it too?"

"She wants it."

"She's using this excuse?"

"No. She's taking this opportunity."

"You think the kid will be happy that I'm there?"

"Of course."

"He and I get along well."

"I know."

"You think it's a way . . . You think I'm missed?"

"Are you talking about the boy?"

"I'm talking about Valentina."

"If she didn't want to see you, she wouldn't have called."

"You think she wants to get back together?"

"I don't know. How did she sound?"

He thinks. Sucks on a forty-eighth mint.

"Distant."

"Well, she's taking a first step."

"You think so?"

"Yes."

"Do we want to be with women again? We're perfectly fine without them."

"We're perfectly fine. Are you still seeing Anne Honoré?"

"Nope. I'm afraid of that Martinican husband."

"Why?"

"He's a brute. Like all those island men are. Look at the Japanese. The Australians! They see an Aborigine, they bring out their cleavers. They're all sons of convicts. I see that Peggy lady every so often. If you could get yourself out of that bath someday, I'd be able to shit."

"Fine."

"I'm seeing other girls, too. They stop by my dump. Every other time I can't pull it off. Every other time, nothing. Fine. The problem is afterwards. Probably the trick's to pretend I'm asleep. If you're lucky you'll hear her get dressed, say something you don't understand, and they close the door quietly. That's a perfect night. You get up, go to the fridge. You tell yourself that's a classy dame. Give me the crossword, will you?"

I hand him the paper. In the bedroom I open the curtains and look out, as if I were looking from another country, on the park in front of the hotel.

∽

A Vieux Campeur shoe in hand, the hotel hair dryer in the other, Serge's lying on the bed, wrapped in a limp, white Radisson bathrobe. He's a genius at wallowing. Nobody can wallow like he does. The dryer screams and stops regularly as he stuffs its bulk into the shoe.

He says, "Do you think my life's a total failure?"

"Why would you say that?"

"Nana doesn't see the least bit of success in my life."

"She said that while she was angry."

"She's right, though."

"You know Ramos is untouchable. Her son, too."

"What a shitty family."

"Enough with that noise, I can't take it anymore!"

"This dryer is a dud."

"Get dressed."

"She knows misery better than Mother Teresa nowadays. Ever since she got that social aid gig, she's gotten all stuck-up. Those people obsessed with virtue signaling sicken me. France has become one of those backward countries because of people like her."

Across the street, going down the sidewalk past the park in a tight, long horde, is a huge group of Israelis carrying Zara and H&M bags.

"We've lain down our weapons of war for a peaceful world rooted in goodwill, self-preservation, and other solidarity pablum. The other day she told me she was *moved to be able to nurture civic pathways*. By text. To me. Actually meant for me."

He drops the dryer and smokes. The ashes fall on the bathrobe. I toss an ashtray at him.

"And cook! I forgot! Nowadays being a chef is better than getting the Nobel. The only one over there who's any good is Margot. And who knows what'll become of her."

"Enough whining. Get up."

"All that raged within me has stilled."

"Should I put on a clean shirt or yesterday's tee?"

"I used to dive in headfirst, I used to laugh at danger, and now all I want is to steer clear of catastrophe. In Auschwitz I would have been a Muselmann in twenty-four hours. I wouldn't have had a single reason to cling to life."

"Clean shirt."

"Give me the room-service menu."

"Come out for a stroll. Kraków's lovely."

"I don't want to spend time with her. I don't want to ever spend time with her again. She was lucky we were at Birkenau."

My phone rings. Paulette. I hear her laugh before she speaks.

"Guess what Maurice's insisting on tonight? An electric walker!"

"Very funny!"

"You know what I said? I said, 'Maurice, you know what's an electric walker? A scooter! Ha ha ha.'"

"Ha ha ha."

"He got a kick out of that, yes, he did! Now he's having his beloved champagne. Where are you all now? Still in Auschwitz?"

"In Kraków."

"Fantastic. You kids have yourselves a great time!"

"Thank you, Paulette."

"*Rice pudding!*" Serge shrieks in English. Then he switches back to French: "You think I should order some rice pudding?"

"Don't be stupid, get up."

"But I love rice pudding. I haven't had rice pudding in ten years."

"We'll find some in a restaurant."

"You know what I like about Isaac Bashevis Singer? The space he makes for those dishes that his guys enjoy. He doesn't tell you what the guy's job is, he tells you what he's wolfing down. Chopped liver, blintzes, even cheesecake, even kugel . . . At one point he goes into a cafeteria in New York, he meets some Polish friends. They talk about Israel and other things, but mainly—wait, I'll read it out loud—'acquaintances who were eating rice pudding or stewed prunes the last time I was here and are already in their graves.' Acquaintances who were eating rice pudding or stewed prunes the last time I was here and are already in their graves. I think about that every day. In my eyes that's as good as a line from the Talmud."

∽

On Kraków's Main Square, the scope of the disaster is striking. There's been some sort of spring festival or music festival or was it a manifestation of those permanent festivities the way there now seems to be in tourist cities? There appears to be everything under the sun in this immense marketplace, a world exactly like the one we saw that very morning in Auschwitz: weary crazed groups with no free will, with bottles and backpacks, but also nuns, Tibetan monks, a long line of white horse-drawn carriages yoked to various horses and driven by cigarette-smoking folks in cowboy outfits. Along the arcades, a rock band makes background music on a huge stage. All the adjoining streets thrum with a similarly feverish, listless, noisy, undifferentiated mass keen on distraction. I'd been to Kraków years ago; what I remember of it is a splendid, clandestine city. Nothing like this fake décor spoiled by a mindless global invasion.

What about you? I wonder as we look, among the dozens of souvenir shops on a crowded pedestrian street, for a local restaurant. What kind of stuff do you think you're made of? You go to and fro across this earth on budget flights just as unthinkingly. You tread the same path: horror at dawn, medieval fair at dusk. You're no different. You don't want to be mistaken for them, but even that unwillingness—a last bit of pride—goes to show what you really are. You know there's no other world anymore and your complaint is just as unthinking.

Lara Fabian's ruined our dinner. As we sit by a stone wall in the tavern basement, the prevailing impression, at first, is of calm. But as the tables around us fill up, the imperceptible trickle of voices from the loudspeaker just above our heads becomes a screaming refrain.

"Lara Fabian," Joséphine says.

I decide to take some interest in her life. She diligently answers my questions with her face half turned toward her father, and I can see that everything she says is to talk her up to him.

"She does makeup," Joséphine explains, "mainly for journalists right before they go on air but also for guests. She does makeup for the rapper KatSé, you know who that is, Papa? No, that's right, you're into rock! She has a nine-week schedule, she does two weeks on a nine-to-five and two weeks with staggered hours. She works completely independently; her head makeup artist is with her in the dressing room but she takes care of administrative stuff and orders cosmetic products from suppliers..."

Serge is busy managing the table—wine, salt, pepper, cornichons—and nods without ever managing to disguise his boredom.

At one point he says, "What about eyebrow training?"

"*Microblading*, Papa. It's the future."

"Three thousand euros, that's how much I paid for that joke."

"Serge!" Nana says, shocked.

"Once I've set up my own salon, I'll pay you back," Jo says, smiling heroically.

Serge tilts his head at the speaker and says, "Can we shut this pig up?"

Nana waves over a waiter. In English, she says, "Please, please mister, could you put the sound lower?" and gestures with her hands to make it happen.

"He needs to turn it off!" Serge insists, not looking at her. "It's a nuisance." Ever since leaving the hotel, he's been busy acting as if she doesn't exist.

"Tell him yourself," Nana says.

"They won't turn off the music for us," Jo says.

Serge switches to English and shouts, "Can you stop the music?"

Everyone's eyes turn to our table. A woman in a traditional flared pea-green skirt like a tutu rushes over. The poor lady tries to explain to us that the music is house policy, that she's all too happy to turn it down slightly but that it's just rotten luck we're at the table under the speakers.

Serge downs an umpteenth glass of vodka and shouts in English, "It's not music, it's noise!" and then adds, "We know her, she is French."

The lady chuckles politely, swishing her skirt, and offers us some blackcurrant liqueur. "Amazing outfit," Serge hisses through his teeth. I ask for the check but Serge wants his rice pudding. When it comes, he deems it too sugary, too vanilla-y, and too soft.

∽

Joséphine's farther off talking with a young American guy. Nana and I sit on Joseph Conrad's bench, Serge is a few meters down the path on the Swiatłana Aleksijewicz bench (that's the Polish spelling). In the park, all the benches have writers' names. Some have nothing to do with Poland. Night has fallen. A few people go by. There's nothing to do in the park.

I tell Nana, "It's touching that you defend your husband so vehemently."

She shrugs. She's bought Polish cigarettes and she's smoking with her lips puckered. Serge's smoking on his bench, too.

She says, "How long's he going to give me that scowl?"

"You hurt his feelings."

"He's totally self-centered."

"Try putting yourself in his shoes."

"I've had enough of putting myself in his shoes. He doesn't put himself in anyone's shoes, does he? We'll square up when we're back. No reason you should have to pay for everyone."

"Leave it be."

"I want to pay for my trip."

"As you like."

"He can't get out of his own head, he can't just be happy. Not for two whole minutes."

"This isn't the best place to be happy."

"Oh, stop it."

"Is that a squirrel I just saw?"

"With this whole Walser thing, I'm standing behind my son one hundred percent. One hundred and fifty percent!"

I give Joséphine and the American boy sitting on another bench a little wave.

"He didn't read the Swiss guy's email. He's shouting down Victor with that whole I'll-show-you-what-life's-like tone and he didn't even read the email! I talked to Victor before dinner. It's utterly humiliating for him to get offered a stage as an apprentice. Unpaid. Like he has no experience! Of course that's how he came off. I'll say it, there's nothing worse than people who only help out to toot their own horn. Victor reacted exactly how he should have. And his project's great, too. It's high time that someone in this family pushed back against Serge."

I laugh. I try to hug her but she pushes me away.

"And this stupid thing you two have against Ramos, it's so childish. And annoying. Why am I smoking? I'll be sick."

She crushes her cigarette under her foot, then changes her mind and, in an environmentally friendly burst, goes to throw it in a trash can. She sits back down and stretches her legs.

"I'm happy I saw Auschwitz, though."

From the Swiatłana Aleksijewicz bench, Serge says, "Three years studying at the so-called best European culinary institute, the Harvard of gastronomy, just to open a fast-food spot!"

"Did he hear everything?" Nana whispers.

"Everything," he says. "Even when you're whispering, I can hear you."

"What a pathetic take! Totally brainless!" Nana shouts in the park's silence. "The better things are, the less I think of you, Serge, and even when it comes to things I thought you were actually good at, when I figure your failure is just bad luck, I can see you don't know shit, you just talk, talk, talk!"

Joséphine and the American guy have turned away.

"All I hear is the bitter sound of your voice, you're full of bitterness and spite and you're turning your back on a twenty-year-old boy who's got a whole life ahead of him and who just might succeed right where you totally failed! Do you even know what fast food means?" Nana spat out the anglicism. "It means 'served quickly,' Serge, not Burger King or any of those vile things, it just means prepared and served quickly, it doesn't mean disgusting. On the contrary. Nowadays, guess what, you can get amazing food in a cardboard box. It's all the rage, in fact. Three years of school to open a fast-food place because that's what's most feasible when one doesn't have much money to put up. Fast food means small business, small stock, small team, small rent, small risk . . . everything's small, yes, but everything's manageable, and if it takes off, mark my words, it'll reap dividends far bigger than those of a bistro. A fast-food spot is the footbath before the full swimming pool, and, I'll say it, I'm proud of how smart my son is, who has to be the most ambitious of us all but who doesn't satisfy himself with hazy hypothetical dreams—he's going to find himself actual ways to succeed. Maybe, deep down, that's pissing you off, seeing someone in this family with real business sense, maybe you're jealous. How sad. So instead of spitting your venom like an old sourpuss, maybe you ought to clap for him and give him some encouragement, that'd get you out of this stifling self-centeredness that you're stuck in and that you stick others in. Because Serge, this is the last time in my life, the very last time I'm going to put up with your moods, waiting twenty minutes for you to actually leave your room, an hour sweating and prowling around a tourist-ridden town with a guy who's sulking like a total brat to find a crappy restaurant where he can shove some crappy rice pudding in his mouth that no one wants except for him!"

"The footbath before the pool, did you come up with that?" I asked. And, believing that a bit of impishness might well put a smile on our faces, I add: "Or was it Ramos's idea?"

She's slapping me. Not gently. Hard. My back, my head, my arm, wherever she can lay her hand.

Joséphine rushes over.

"What's going on?"

Nana gets up, her nostrils flaring, red and steaming.

"I can't stand your father any longer! Or him," she fumes, shoving me away, "or anyone else. I hate you all!"

Serge says to Jo, "See where your idea of a pilgrimage has gotten us."

Nana grabs her bag and strides off.

"Where's she headed? Where are you going? The Radisson's over that way!" I shout. She spins around. As she walks past us like a Fury, I ask, "What time are we leaving tomorrow morning?"

She doesn't respond.

"Nana!"

Her voice in the distance is barely audible: "Fuck off."

∽

"You know that with Jews," Serge says, sprawled out in a plush chair at the Radisson, "when you walk by a beggar, you have to give him something, you *have* to. It's a mitzvah. An obligation. And you know why you *have* to? Not out of charity, not to be nice. Not so the guy can eat, no. You *have* to so you don't end up telling yourself a few meters later, damn I should have given him three euros, or if you did, damn what a great guy I am. Not because it's the sin of pride like with Catholics, no. Because it's a waste of time. You *have* to give so you don't get saddled with pesky considerations. That lets you skip the whole question of whether or not to do it. The path's straightforward and your brain doesn't waste time with silliness. Jews are geniuses."

We get one last drink at the bar. Several last drinks, rather. Joséphine has headed out with the Jew from Seattle. Up above, a screen on the wall broadcasts CNN on mute. Trump's done-up hair pulls away from his scalp in a backward bulge where the part is. I wonder if his hair stylist uses a BaByliss. I spent ages one time watching Marion shaping her curls with that tool.

"Do you give to the poor?" I ask.

"Here and there. But when I give something, I can't help congratulating myself after."

He grabs a handful of chips.

"Categorical imperatives. No choice. That's my ideal life. Do I offload the car lot on some patsy I know and trust? No. Do I sell the shop? No. Do I get a checkup? Do I try to win Valentina back? Do I fall out with Nana and the whole Ochoa family or do I forgive them? Do I go into debt again for Jo's apartment?"

"Why would you get a checkup?"

"Because I'm that age. At my age you get a checkup."

"Who's the patsy?"

"Jacky's brother-in-law."

"You think it's better to sell it?"

"It's a gas factory. The commissioner won't do a single thing without a public comment period. When I read 'public comment', I know it's hopeless. Chiche can say whatever he likes, if we have to wait for elected representatives, locals, environmental associations, the prefecture, the communes, *vaffanculo*! But so long as the prospect of building still looks feasible on paper, I can play for time."

We order another ginger vodka. Serge goes to turn the lampshade.

"The footbath before the pool, that's Ramos," I say.

"Of course it is. The way she reacted to that, you know it's him. Who else would say such a thing?"

"The footbath before the pool . . ."

"Ha ha ha!"

"They must have had a little family discussion . . ."

"They absolutely must have."

"When you've never swum before you don't jump right into the big pool . . ."

"She gave you a real beating for that, didn't she! Ha ha ha." Then he sets down his glass and pulls Luc's scowling chestnut out of his pocket.

"You still have that? You brought it?!"

"I'll never abandon it."

The thing touches me far more than it ought to.

"I'll tell Luc."

He runs his thumb over the chestnut, which already has cracks in it.

∽

At one in the morning, he gets worried and calls Jo on her phone.

"Answering machine! What does she think she's doing! That girl's going to ruin my night! Uh, hello. It's me. Where are you, Jo? Call me back, please."

I remind him that Jo is an independent adult who's been living as she sees fit for ages.

"She'll spend the night with a stranger? But she doesn't know the guy!"

"The night? Serge, it's one o'clock."

"Why doesn't she keep her phone on? In an unfamiliar city! What's this girl got in her head?"

"Don't be stupid."

"I can't go to sleep if I don't know where she is."

"Send her a text. On WhatsApp. Tell her that we're leaving the hotel at seven. The plane's at ten."

"All right . . ."

I get up.

"Come on. You're not going to get anything else done here."

"Hang on, hang on. I'm going to wait here a bit longer. You moved the lamp, put it back. The lampshade! The other way, the other way!"

"Why are you so wound up?"

"I didn't like the looks of that man. A Jew from Seattle? You know that's druggy town."

"He looked like a nice boy."

"Those are the worst. The most dangerous criminals look harmless."

"Come on, Serge."

"Did we need to go to Auschwitz? Be honest. Did we need the whole gang? Maybe it will end in tragedy."

He takes out a blue pill and swallows it.

"How many of those are you taking every day? I'm tired of waiting for you. Come on."

He gets up unwillingly. The bartender's in a hurry to close up. We go a short way. In front of the elevator Serge says, "Let's have a quick look outside." We head out, the street's calm, lit only at the park's edges. He lights a cigarette. A shadow pops up at the intersection. "It's her!" Serge rushes over toward the figure, a frail little man in his sixties without much of a torso, wearing a short-sleeve shirt tucked into pleated Bermuda shorts. The sort of guy you only see around Austria. Up close, we notice that he's wearing a ribbon around his neck with a huge medal hanging off it. The man greets us in Polish and goes on his way.

"How could you have thought that was Jo?"

"I panicked!"

In the empty lobby he collapses into a multicolored chair. I do likewise in another. A night manager comes and goes through a small door behind the front desk. The dimmed ceiling lights tinge everything green. Every so often one of the fluorescent tubes flickers.

A day along the train tracks. Tracks that look no different from other tracks. Railroads through the countryside just like anywhere else in the world. Obsolete tracks, crushed stones where grass springs up that needs to be weeded, strips of steel quietly kept clean, crossties. Tracks, railroads, tracks, railroads. Nana with her red messenger bag in front of the empty platform. Nanny Miro walking along the Birkenau tracks in her coat. Nanny Miro who I hadn't thought about in years and who comes to mind with a single image. Until I was eight our mother had worked four days a week as a clerk at Martine & Belle on rue Saint-Honoré. A very old woman watched us, she had a short gray haircut that was round and soft and she came and left on the bus. We didn't know anything about her life, or where she lived, or if she had a husband or children. We knew she was born in the Jura. She was simple and devoted, always happy to see us—she was of a simplicity that still touches me and that I think highly of. She had a flimsy bag she pulled little presents out of, candy or pictures. For our first few years, she was our real mother. One day we didn't see her again. We were back from vacation, our parents said she'd gone back home. When I think of the word *Jura*, I see isolated structures and fortresses in ruins in an arid landscape. I don't see trees in the Jura. We never found out what had happened to her, we never knew anything about her apart from her name. Germaine Miro disappeared, swallowed up by chance and the paths of dull hills.

I didn't know how I should steer myself emotionally through these realms of cosmic names, Auschwitz and Birkenau. I waver between coldness and a quest for emotion that amounts to a certificate of good behavior. In any case, I tell myself, aren't all these do-you-remembers, these angry appeals to memory just as much subterfuges to smooth over the event and set them, in good conscience, in history? Long live Cerezo!

Around two in the morning, Joséphine appears through the revolving doors. She sees us slumped like two hobos in the glum light.

"What are you doing here?!"

"Your father thought you were dead."

"Jo! My girl, there you are! Thank the lord, thank the lord! Come here, my Joséphine, come into my arms, come into your father's arms!"

Jo comes and sits in her father's lap as he hugs her, blustering. She gives me a bewildered look. And she stays put. Her head on her father's shoulders. Her huge body oddly overwhelming his. After some time, she says, "Lara Fabian isn't French, Papa. She's Belgian."

I don't even have it in me to get up and go to bed.

༄

In Paris, Zita is waiting for me at her place in a long green quilted bathrobe, whiskey in hand. On the phone she's informed me that on top of her two femurs and her osteoporosis, not to mention her thyroid, she now has cancer of some gland.

"Doctor's orders," she insists as she lights a Chesterfield. "I've got the prescription here. See: a glass of brandy in the evening. He wrote brandy because I said brandy but it could be Scotch, doesn't matter. He likes me. I'm his favorite. He also wants me to walk with my crutches, see, it says: 'Walk to the boulangerie and back.' He knows I like their poppy-seed cakes. Now that's the dream. A little walk with my crutches, Doc, 'you wake up and your hand's dangling in the chamber pot,' I told him. It's a Hungarian expression. They made your mother do the exercise bike, poor thing. An exercise bike! Why do they want us moving around before the grave? But he gets me. I said, 'Doc, no pain. Death if you want, but make it easy. None of those stupid meds and no pain.' Remember my poor Max, who was tossing and turning in his bed and that shithead city doctor kicking up a fuss with his packs of morphine? Tell me, do I look like a madwoman with my hair all over the place? Antoninos's retired. She had the guts but not the know-how. Now I've got a Vietnamese girl, a youngster with modern tastes. And she's a manicurist too! She donates to that Jewish appeal charity because she does the president's hands and he asked her, 'Did you donate this year, Anh Dào? Those bandits set fire to everything.' When Max died, I kept Romanian orphans, cancer, multiple sclerosis, hunger, and poverty, all that, but I got rid of all the Jewish associations. They pester you, they keep nagging at you, those leeches. Even now some of them are trying to get me back on board. The synagogue in Calcutta is entirely made of marble thanks to Max. There's sixty of them. I know he's mad at me. With your father, it was Israel. He got fleeced by Israel. He gave to the army, to irrigation programs, God knows what. When he died, Marta put a stop to it all. But Edgar kept on guilt-tripping her. He'd come to her at night: 'Why aren't you giving to Yad

Vashem anymore?' He gave her hell and she'd wake up feeling guilty. It's so sweet of you to waste your time with this old body. What do you do again? Are you still doing that—I forget what it is you do, my dear."

"I'm a materials conductivity specialist."

"Oh yeah! You were always a genius!"

"Right."

"Living as a shut-in doesn't bother me that much, you know. On the contrary. I don't have to deal with nuisances anymore. I'm not suffering, apart from the usual aches and pains. In the evening, I open the window, I hear life going on, the young people walking by. Marta married a pain in the ass who wouldn't age gracefully. No one does. Especially not Jews. We can say that now. Edgar was a pain in the ass, and a wet blanket too. She had a little fling with André Ponchon."

"André Ponchon!"

"You know at some point a woman will eventually come around."

"But not with André Ponchon!"

"Even with him. When a man sticks around long enough, women eventually come to their senses. A bad husband, three kids—you take what you can get, my boy. Don't try to paper over that. Everyone's six feet under, we don't care. Now, tell me about Maurice. What's the latest with him? Don't tell him what I've been dealing with. Tell him I'm getting out, going to concerts, still classy in high heels, tell me you saw me in Rubi Palatino's arms! Ha ha ha. No, he won't believe that, not to mention that

Rubi's dead too, unless he isn't, I've been burying everyone, but if he isn't dead then how old has he got to be now?"

"Who's Rubi?"

"Rubi Palatino, looks exactly like Porfirio Rubirosa, all the girls were mad about him. A customer's husband came and threatened him in his leather goods store on rue de Provence with a hunting gun. Now, I won't be cremated like your mother. No. After I saw that horrible room, that rathole with Marta all alone in her coffin, I changed my mind. I want up and out. A little ceremony outside in Bagneux and poof. Max's daughter asked me if I wanted their rabbi to come. He did everything in their family—bar mitzvah, their kids' bris, their parents' funerals. If it makes Max happy for him to come, let him. What difference does it make?"

∽

That minds can be changed based on the same facts is just as common a matter as it's worrying.

Six months ago, the fake Argentine was a man of great virility, almost even modern virility, a man to whom that dusty idea never would have occurred to pay for the hotel room, let alone the restaurant—he just accepted pampering and gifts with manly simplicity. "A free man," Marion said, in a fit that I can't even describe.

Nowadays, dressed like a maid and ironing a heap of clothes, she says, "It's terrifying, this guy turns fifty and can't even buy his mistress a boat trip! He doesn't blink twice at being invited along. That's normal life for him. On Lac Daumesnil I was digging through my bag for my wallet, and he'd already sat down with his sleeves rolled up and oars in hand! Who raised him? No flowers. Not even a little attempt. He's a grubby little rat. I pity his wife! No wonder she wants to divorce him."

"You thought he was pretty manly," I say.

"For other reasons."

"No, no, you thought he was manly because a woman in love is a total idiot."

"And a man isn't?"

"Not as much."

She rolls her eyes. I do like it when she's fed up. As a jet of steam rises, she says, "Now I just find him pathetic."

"Are you going to leave him?"

She thinks, starts on a fitted sheet that she can't get properly on the ironing board.

"You aren't going to stay with a pathetic man, Marion."

"Show me a guy who isn't pathetic."

Luc slips through the apartment like a shadow. He's up against the walls, wary of hidden enemies.

I hesitate to say "me." It would be stupid to say "me."

"Me," I say.

"You!" She bursts out laughing.

"Yes, I know, it's funny."

"You just make me unhappy. And you're the one who left me. And you're pathetic, too."

Luc holds a finger up to his lips so I don't betray his presence. I point discreetly at the kitchen, where the threat seems to be coming from. He freezes, on alert.

"What will he do for the school thing?"

"Something Italian. I haven't found out whether he's supposed to be a soccer fan or a gondolier."

"A gondolier, he's seen those in Venice."

"I'm not the one who decides. You like my boobs?"

"Absolutely."

"You don't think I need to get a boob job?"

"What ever got that idea in your head? Was it that moron?"

"They're drooping."

With a furtive jump, Luc reaches the kitchen doorway and presses his shoulder to the jamb.

I say to Marion, "How about if we go to the garden? It's not raining anymore."

"You think they're drooping!"

"Not at all! And so what if they're drooping? That's sexy. You don't need a teenager's boobs."

"Fine. Let's go to the garden."

The Bègues public garden is on the grounds of the former Conservatoire des Écluses. A mysterious realm, sloping downward and dotted with old wooden benches.

Luc zigs and zags through the bushes and trees. He speaks quietly with an ally he's sending coded signals to.

A small army of gulls contemplates the statue of Leda intertwined with her swan on the forbidden lawn. A child in red overalls pops up and delights in running at them. All the gulls flap away and settle down elsewhere. The child, unbothered by rules and regulations, chases after them again.

Marion tells me the story of one of her colleagues, who called the website where she buys her dry cat food. "The food's no good," her colleague said, "my cat's thirsty after eating it."

"What flavor is it?" the lady on the other end of the line said.

"No idea," the colleague said.

"Is the food the flavor she usually eats?"

"Ma'am, I'm not eating it myself."

"Can you send us back the package?"

"Sure."

"But the package has to be unopened."

"Okay, sure, I can close it back up," the colleague said.

"No, the package can't have been opened already."

Marion and I have a laugh. It's nice out. I give her a kiss. She says, "Maybe I should get Luc a pet, a rabbit for the apartment or a parrot."

"Why not a dog or a cat?"

"I'm scared of cats. And a dog—who'd walk it?"

We walk around the rectangular basin. Luc runs ahead, arms outstretched.

Marion says, "Sometimes I think the three of us ought to live together."

It's the moment to say something decisive. But nothing comes. I don't know if it's because I don't have the words or because my mind's suddenly gone into a panic, or some mysterious part of myself that's gone dead.

I think she's not wrong to consider me pathetic.

∽

Now that we're all back from Auschwitz, Nana and Serge have independently and mutually decided not to talk to each other ever again. I have to listen to their respective complaints, each of them fundamentally trying to paint the other as objectively to be avoided and to convince me that, were it not my brother (or my sister), I'd be better off not seeing him (or her). They each try to win me over. My stance of not taking sides only makes things worse and gets me called a coward who's never had a kid and doesn't know what it's like, a guy who's passive or weak or defensive without any real family values.

As odd as that might seem, the last detail isn't unfounded. Our family bookshelf was small and outdated. It took up a small stretch of the wall in the front hall on rue Pagnol and among obscure treatises, chess magazines, various books on Israel and its exploits, biographies of Golda Meir, Menachem Begin, and esoteric things like L. Ron Hubbard's *Dianetics*, there turned out to be a few novels. I don't think I read anything but comics before I was a teen. But I always did like looking at and touching the books. I liked the titles. The titles were enough, they gave a glimpse of other worlds, even if I got the wrong idea. My favorites when I went to the front hall looking for a dose of sadness were Hector Malot's *Alone in the World* and Alphonse Daudet's *Little What's-His-Name*, and also, although not as much because I couldn't really connect with it, Musil's *The Confusions of Young Törless*. All books of misfortune. But not just any misfortune. Books of abandonment, of being orphaned. Being alone in the world and without family struck me as one and the same thing, as the most unenviable condition of existence. Has something of that remained? Are my attempts to restore our sibling bonds tied up in that old framework?

As I walk to my class at Saclay, he calls. To all his other faults I have to add terrible phone karma. Even if I have no idea what, for him, would constitute good phone karma. The bus is coming. He wants to see me. To cut to the chase, I agree to see him that night at a café by my place. As soon as I hang up, I regret it. In the RER, I almost call him back to postpone. I wonder: why bother, though? Why change things when you can't get out of the meeting in the end? Why don't I have the courage to claim psychological unavailability, to draw on some sort of post-Auschwitz neurasthenia? But of course. Could I still do that? It'd be a pointless complication! All that time wasted! Is there some sort of categorical imperative for such circumstances? A mitzvah when it comes to a Ramos Ochoa?

He's in front of me. Slumped shoulders and crestfallen face. His hair's grown, white corkscrews that refuse to coil alongside the others. He strikes me as ruddy. Has he been drinking already? He orders some chardonnay. I get a Perrier with lemon. He wets his lips with the yellow liquid and licks them. I remove the peel from the lemon and drop it in the water. He takes out a handkerchief and blows his nose noisily. "Pollen," he says. He asks if I found the trip to be nourishing. That's the word he used. All of which means I'm tense from the outset. I tell him I hadn't had any particular expectations for the trip and that I hadn't fully thought through its implications yet. "Nana came back distraught." I nod. He'd get to the point. But I've forgotten who I'm with—he's in no rush. An absurd silence falls. We just sit.

He finally says, with a glassy stare, "You're mistreating her. Why?"

"What'd she tell you?" I spit out, unthinkingly.

"She told me everything. Including what you said about me."

"Oh, we were teasing each other!" I chuckle.

"I don't work in the civil service. I have no safety net."

"I know that."

"Show me a fixed-term contract, I'll take it."

"Ramos, be smarter than her. We were joking, you know us."

"I do know you, but that's not the point." His voice is glottal, calm, and terribly still.

I'd recently learned that he was making sandwiches for the hobos downstairs.

"Fine. Is that why you wanted to see me?"

He swirls his glass. His head bobs. As if he wished he hadn't dropped the topic so quickly.

"First," he says, taking an unthinkable amount of time, "I want you to know that Victor's fusion fast-food project is incredible. And don't just take my word for it."

"I have no doubt of it."

"He presented his business plan to his go-to chef who, by the way, was named Best Worker in France. The man told him, straight out, 'If you open it, I'll invest in it.' The pastry chef next to him said, 'So will I.' As for the management professor, he confirmed that the model was more than viable."

"That's really something."

At this point I'm certain this isn't his first glass.

"He might not have much education . . ."

"Ramos, you don't have to . . ."

"But I've raised a businessman. That kid is a businessman. Not an employee."

"No."

"When I was his age, I had wings too. But I didn't have ins."

"Uh huh."

He knocks back his Chardonnay and waves for it to be refilled. I order some Côtes du Rhône.

"A mother can't have her son being bad-mouthed. And for no good reason. And by her own brother. You can't ask that of a mother."

"She stood up for him," I say. "She stood up for Victor. She didn't take it lying down."

"It was too much for her."

"Oh, don't exaggerate."

"She isn't sleeping anymore. She's on edge. Yesterday she chewed me out because I was rinsing the salad too slowly and then she burst into tears after she poured the pot of pasta out by the dish rack."

"Maybe you do rinse the salad too slowly . . ."

"She's out of sorts, she's unhappy."

"And what are you hoping I'll do?"

"You need to convince Serge to apologize."

"Ramos, right now, Serge is waiting for an apology from Victor."

"Victor won't be apologizing for anything because he has nothing to apologize for," he says a bit too loudly.

"Let's not get involved, then."

"Nana's right, you're Serge's yes-man."

I didn't get to contemplate the overfamiliarity (and impertinence) of that line because my phone was vibrating. Maurice!

"Excuse me," I say, "it's Maurice."

"Hello?"

"Maurice?"

A man's voice sings "*Ochi Chyornye*," then Paulette's voice shrieks into the receiver: "Can you hear it? He's had his beloved champagne and now he's singing!"

"Yes, yes, I hear it . . ."

I switch it to speakerphone for Ramos. Even when diminished, Maurice's voice is as sharp and passionate as an old man's can be . . .

"*Ochi zhguchiye, ochi strastnye . . .*"

Ramos stares at the phone fearfully. Maurice is singing the entirety of "*Ochi Chyornye*." At the end, I clap, I say, "Magnificent!"

There's audible, insane gurgling.

"Great, we'll leave you be," Paulette says.

Ramos asks, "How's he doing?"

"He's bedridden."

He nods, bewildered.

"We've got that coming ourselves . . ."

He blows his nose and rubs his eyes. I observe his heavy lower eyelids. I'd never noticed what heavy bags he has under them. I feel tenderness rise up, the sort of highly suspect tenderness that we feel when men show signs of melancholy. Could this Ramos be a brave man? A brave, maladjusted man trying to hold onto the reins of his life?

"And what are we doing? We're wasting time tearing each other to pieces!" he says. "We're old. We're too old for these squabbles."

There he is again. And that idiot thinks he can get one over on me.

I say, "Everyone I know bickers until they're on their last legs. And after, too."

He nods.

"She's your little sister," he says as he takes a sip.

"Why aren't you calling Serge directly? Why are you going through me?"

"Because you're normal."

"Oh, how wonderful!"
"You're the only one with a level head."
"Are you blind or what?"

∽

There's no debate: ravens, crows, pigeons, and possibly ducks love rue Grèze. They're everywhere. On the awning of the Honoré-Pain on the corner, on the rooftops and the daycare's security fence, on the low wall and in the treetops of the Association des Cultures Francophones, they chatter on the sidewalks and flit off disdainfully to make space for passersby. The inhabitants have special meetings and get quotes that often go nowhere. Hence this morning's email:

Having spoken with Madame Lupesco, who expressed frustration at the pigeon droppings, you'll find attached two quotes. The first is for the woman's windowsills: this quote will resolve part of the issue because the pigeons land on the sill of the shutters where we cannot do anything; the solution will be to change her shutters for sliding or folding shutters. The second has to do with the zinc roof, because while I was speaking with Madame Lupesco, we saw a woman from the trade-union council and both of them wanted a quote for spikes on the whole roof. I told them that I'm not in favor of these sorts of spikes, because they get dirty quickly— things catch on them right away (plastic bags, leaves, rags, etc.); if work has to be done on the roof then that complicates matters significantly; and also some fellow owners simply won't live face-to-face with an array of spikes.

Sincerely,

Antonio Sanchez
KAKOR
PEST EXTERMINATION AND DISINFECTION

"Some fellow owners": that's me. I can't stand the sight of spikes. Never mind that on rue Grèze, birds do as they like. What's remarkable is how they can't stay put anywhere. They're driven by some sort of feverish impatience, an unquenchable thirst for new observation posts. I'd like to say "new activity," but they just land to fly off to land elsewhere, flit away from a balustrade to land on the facing one and vice versa, hop on the road to end up on the sidewalk, follow such and such a gutter, dive into a chimney and come back out to land on the gutter. No rhyme or reason, no rest for them. A fear of stillness. A horror of downtime. I think of Thomas Bernhard, who went to Nathal to recover from Vienna, left for Vienna to recuperate from Nathal, back and forth at diminishing intervals, with fleeting stops in other towns with promising names, defining himself in a splendid line: "When I arrive, no matter where, I am suddenly the unhappiest person imaginable," which always made me think of Serge, unable to enjoy being somewhere without immediately wishing not to be there, claiming all his life to need to "save himself." Father used to say, "He's fidgety, always happier elsewhere!" It didn't bode well in his eyes. All he saw in this fitfulness was insanity or illness. I myself never thought it was mere fretting. Birds aren't fretful or fitful or full of folly. They try to find the best spot and never do. Everyone thinks there's a better spot.

∾

I'm in his Champ de Mars apartment. A dark, conventional one-bedroom with a few masterstrokes like turquoise leopard-print cushions. "Did Seligmann do the decoration?" I ask.

"Who knows."

No trace of Serge's presence anywhere apart from the nightstand with the shattered Ganesha in a small bowl, half-used blister packs of medicine, and some books. In the main room, a plant, supported by a gray PVC tube serving as a stake and hooks under the molding, climbs along the window and under the ceiling. Whitish star-shaped flowers clustered in an umbel seem to produce a sap dripping onto the ground.

"What a ghastly plant," I say.

"Shit," Serge blurts out. "I forgot to water it!"

He goes into the kitchen and comes back with a plastic watering can that has a long, curved spout. Then he takes a sponge and tackles the stains the liquid's left on the parquet.

"Why don't you toss it? Such a disgusting thing."

"I can't."

"Why not?"

"It's a protective being."

"Really? How'd you figure that out?"

"Patrick. He tried to get rid of it but the plant made it clear that it wasn't going anywhere."

In the early two thousands, I learned, while he was putting the finishing touches on the floor with a trowel, Patrick Seligmann moved in with Lucie Lapiower, a regular at the record shop. Lucie's parents had, among other things, gifted her this plant, a plant they'd raised from seed and watched grow in their shoe store. Patrick quickly took a dislike to it, but Lucie insisted on keeping it so as not to upset her parents. Patrick decided to kill it discreetly by watering it with bleach. He used small amounts at first out of fear of being caught out by the smell, only to use more and more. The plant was unaffected. Patrick grew bolder. He poured drain cleaner and all-purpose cleaner in. The plant didn't move. It actually seemed to prosper up high, such that Lucie's parents stopped by one evening with a drill and tools to help it climb up the wall. Patrick decided to clip its roots. As he prepared, he got scared of burning his hands with the corrosive liquids, put on household gloves, and snipped with kitchen scissors at what seemed to be a thick root. The plant grew like magic. He watered it with boiling water. It steamed up but nothing happened. A friend who knew some spells suggested a garlic pod at the bottom of the pot. His own mother said, "Absolutely no garlic! It fortifies!" Lucie fell in love with a racing cyclist and moved to Perpignan, leaving her whole life behind. At this point, Patrick didn't see the plant with the same eyes anymore. It was an evil spirit best left alone. A voice deep down told him not to abandon it. He transplanted it easily enough to an apartment on the Champ de Mars. When he lent it out to Serge, he gave him the story in broad strokes and changed "evil spirit" to "protective being."

That's the story. At least what I get from Serge's telling of it.

"Seligmann's as loony as you are," I say. "Takes one to know one."

"He's not nearly as bad."

He's sitting on the brown couch. He sets one of the leopard-print cushions in his lap and starts patting then smoothing it out with his palm.

"So," he says after a while, still busy with the flattening, "when I got back from Auschwitz I went to the cardiologist. The bicycle stress test came back normal. The electrocardiogram came back normal. The echocardiogram, though, nothing was right: aortic heart murmur and dilation. He tells me, 'The murmur is weak but an aortic dilation can be serious. And especially when it's at the aortic arch, which is a difficult area to operate on.' 'OPERATE?!' 'No, no, not at this stage. The dilation isn't too bad but it needs to be monitored closely, because beyond a particular diameter there could be a rupture.' Meaning: death." He goes back to patting the cushion. "He had me get a scan. The radiologist said forty-seven millimeters' dilation at the aortic root, the same as at the cardiologist's . . ."

"Stop it with your cushion!"

"Fine. So, it's definitely dilated. And he says, on top of that, there's a blotch on your lung. That needs to get checked out in three months in case it moves. That's the assessment." He leaves the cushion with me. "I go in with nothing and I come out with three things. A murmur, a dilation, and a nodule in my lung."

We sit in silence.

"Did you see a doctor after the scan?"

"A pulmonologist. Who said the same thing. It could be nothing or it could be doom. Have to see in three months. I've got an appointment."

"A healthy dose of Xénotran?" I say to lighten the mood. I'm just about to ask for one myself.

"No more than usual. A new magic ritual, though. Conversations with the plant."

"You're talking to it?"

"Of course."

"I don't know about this plant."

"Last night I ate a whole chocolate bar. I did put two squares in the fridge. Want them?"

"Nah."

"I used to be invincible. Everything's gone to pieces now."

It's been ages since I felt such heaviness. In the dark rathole overlooking the dark side street without any sign of life where huge chestnut trees only underscore the sepulchral vibe, I suddenly feel wiped out.

He gets up and comes back with a huge rectangular box on which I read, on the side of a yellow crane against the backdrop of an American city, *SUPER CRANE, Superpowerful*.

"Electric construction crane, for Marzio! It's a meter tall. Remote-controlled. A hundred euros, on sale at La Grande Récré."

I wonder if Marzio will be as happy as Serge clearly is.

"You think I should gift wrap it?"

"Wouldn't be a bad idea. A hundred euros?"

"Yes, it's a bit much. But I didn't want to look bad, you know. Can't show up with a bad present."

"Have you two been talking?"

"We text. Now I'm worried Valentina will think it's too big. She's crazy about tidiness."

He lights a cigarette.

Along with the matches, he takes out Luc's chestnut. He puts it back in his pocket.

"His birthday is Saturday the twelfth. Marzio's bedroom is small. She'll complain because it's too big, I just know it."

"Know what I thought? Tell me if you think it's a terrible idea. Luc's the same age as Marzio, I've been wondering if they should meet . . ."

"Sure, why not."

"All right . . . he's in his own little world, though. Introverted. He doesn't have that many friends. I'm wondering, maybe it's not a good idea, if he couldn't come to Marzio's birthday."

"Give Valentina a call. I'm sure she'll say yes."

"What do you think? That'd mean I have to come too. Luc's shy, he won't go by himself."

"Oh, come! Come! I can't stand the thought of the birthday myself. If you're there it'll be better."

"I haven't called her since you two split . . . No, it's a terrible idea, forget it."

"No, no! You've got to bring the kid! I'll call her myself."

"If she doesn't seem keen, then don't push it. It's just a thought I had."

"Yes, of course."

We fall silent. He snuffs his cigarette in a turquoise cup and grabs another that he twiddles between his fingers. On the varnished coffee table is nothing but this cup and the crane in its huge box.

"I should have gotten it wrapped," he finally says. "I was tired of standing in line. Any news from the Ochoas?"

I say no.

"Is that moron really setting up a fast-food business?"

"Probably."

"Joséphine got dumped by the Tunisian guy. Good riddance."

"You sure you need to smoke?"

"I'm sure."

I get the impression that the plant's producing a new droplet of its sticky liquid.

I had planned to tell him what I'd learned from Zita about André Ponchon. A man from a past where there had been nothing. I was already looking forward to it. But I don't have the courage now, I don't have the energy for such lightheartedness. So André Ponchon goes back where he came from, a shapeless figure disintegrating like gray sand.

∽

My phone rings just before six in the morning. Each night I turn it off or put it in airplane mode. But not last night. Forgetfulness or a sign. It's Paulette. Maurice is dead. She's oddly calm, almost cold.

She says, "He had a coughing fit. He suffocated. Naturally."

"Were you there?"

"No. I was with the night nurse." Her voice drops. "One of those huge Caribbean ladies."

"Where are you?"

"With him. She called me." Her voice drops again. "She said, 'Monsieur Sokolov has passed away.' Her voice was so soft that I couldn't understand her."

"Paulette, I have an onsite with clients from India, I can't be there until tonight."

"His son's coming."

"From Boston?"

"From Tel Aviv." She lets out an abrupt whimper. "He's like a baby! In his little bed with bars all around! We were expecting it, but naturally . . ."

"Yes, Paulette, I know. Take care. See you tonight."

∽

So the world is now bereft of Maurice.

The world that my eyes see, my bedroom where shutters already let through a little light, rue Grèze, rue Raffet, Israel, Russia, the sky, the world from now is one without cousin

Maurice. Maurice Sokolov completed his little trip from cradle to grave without a single soul, himself included, understanding its point.

"For what reason had she lived? And why did she die?" When I was little, I used to repeat to myself those words that Sholem Aleichem had repeated in his most heartbreaking story. Creature had died. No more joy, no more summer. "What does that mean, 'died'?" No more running, singing, frolicking in the river with her friends. Why had she lived? Why had she died?

And despite my belief that he might already be buried in some recess of my brain, I find myself thinking anew of Maurice's lifelong friend Serge Makovsky, long since dead, a joyous, silly giant who reached the end of the line in a loneliness so anguished and dark that no medicine could bring him solace. I hear him again, with his Russian accent, turning up unshaven yet again at this restaurant, I must have been fifteen: "I'm down in the doldrums morning noon and night, I'm down in the doldrrrums, the dooooooldrrrrrums." For years I could remember the dreadful sound coming out of that colossus's mouth and the resulting image of shattered things and bodies: "I'm DOWN, DOWN IN THE DOOOLDRRRRRRUMS."

So I hoist up my body in this new world where Maurice no longer lives. I putter in the bathroom, I draw the bath thinking about how his name won't come up on my phone again, rue Raffet won't crop up again. No more beloved champagne and stamping foot. No more astrakhan hat or sunhat in the summer, no more Sheraton, no more Raffles, no more harebrained women banging at bedroom doors in the night.

You fell through the trapdoor of death, Maurice. You didn't make it to a hundred.

∽

It's true that he's shrunken. Lying in a pink shirt, under a white sheet pulled up to his belt buckle, is a Maurice we've never seen before, his hair neatly combed back. The embalmer's smoothed the old guy out like a long wax doll.

Paulette lets us into the bedroom, carefully shutting the door behind her. "On account of drafts," she says, with a wink clarifying her intent to protect us from Cyril, Maurice's son, by not letting him in as we say our goodbyes. The shutters are closed. On the table for the medical bed are just two scented candles whose flames dance gently. In the cab that brought us there, Serge said, "I've gone all the way to Poland, I've been in Birkenau, and I've never bothered to set foot in rue Raffet." He hadn't seen Maurice in over a year. The last time had to be our hospital visit after his fall at Dyadya Vanya.

Maurice greeted us stretched on his rack, plastered, bandaged, and half-suspended.

"How are you feeling?" Serge had asked, bent over the body with a despondent look.

"I've never felt so good in my life," Maurice answered.

Ever since Maurice's return to rue Raffet to face his dreary existence as an impotent man, ever since his panorama was reduced to his bedroom and his corduroy sofa, Serge had ignored him. He called the elder man exactly once, when Maurice was asleep. He never called again. Even after Auschwitz, he hadn't come, as he'd decided, but the difference, he told me, slumped in the cab, was that he thought about the man every day, he'd even planned to bring him the CD of Dina Ugorskaja performing Beethoven's Opuses 109 and 110, which Maurice had randomly heard on the radio two years earlier, and which he had said that only an exiled Russian Jew of such beauty could play with such a mix of humor and interiority, but he hadn't ordered the CD, hung up by so little time, so many obligations, so much of a mental block, namely, his nauseating selfishness, he told me in the cab.

In the bedroom we fall silent. Each side of the bed's rails are now lowered. Back to mind comes the lively descent down the Champs-Élysées behind the stout man in a camel-hair coat; we'd stretched our legs as far as we could to stay behind him, all the way to Le Normandie, where Kirk Douglas awaited us with an Eskimo. Might Serge, too, be reliving this utterly joyful trip?

A single image can be enough to hold onto a whole man.

∾

In the sitting room, Paulette serves the beloved champagne. Sitting on the corduroy couch, in front of the massive, vaguely erotic reproduction of François Boucher's *L'Odalisque*, are Maddie, Maurice's third wife; Tamara Blum, now a little scamp with mauve hair; and Yolanda, the pretty night nurse.

"Come and have a seat, boys!" Paulette commands us. The boys being us, the physical therapist, and Cyril Sokolov. The women shift over to make space. A few yellowed silk shades with dangling cords let through some dizzying light.

"You do know Monsieur and Madame Fonseca, who saved our life," Paulette says, gesturing to the remaining two seats. Ensconced in two faux-Louis XVI chairs pushed together, the landlord and landlady get up and greet us.

Cyril must be about Serge's age, but his typically American haircut immediately marks him out as one of those patched-up old fogies. Only Americans, I think, would have this hazelnut-dyed pouf on top set off in a clear line from white temples and sideburns. Nothing about him reminds me of his father; he's an unremarkable, paunchy fellow from God knows where. (I couldn't possibly recognize his mother. We caught sight of her once at his wedding in Tel Aviv.) He's sitting on a separate chair that's higher than the sofa. He thanks Serge and me for coming, for taking such good care of his father, especially in this horrible final year (Serge, wedged between Tamara and Maddie, stammers something to extricate himself from the compliment, but Cyril doesn't hear him), he says that Maurice loved us so much, that he spoke highly of us, and so on. Anyone who heard him would think father and son had been thick as thieves, both made of the same stuff that all those kilometers had only brought closer together.

Maddie asks if he's happy at his new job. She hasn't heard a thing!

"Very," he answers, scarfing down an olive. And to satisfy everyone's curiosity, he does his best to explain in detail just what his expertise in evaluating businesses consists of. Tamara and Maddie nod valiantly at his mentions of "external growth" or "divestment projects," and when he gets to his deep involvement in matters of "responsible, sustainable management," he thrusts his chin forward to mimic Bill Clinton's look of humble contentment. "Oh, my dear Paulette!" he sighs, grabbing her shoulders. "Wherever do you find these olives?"

Serge asks his seatmates if he can smoke.

"I'd rather you didn't," Cyril says, "I've had asthmatic attacks since my latest divorce."

"A Casanova, just like his father!" Maddie says.

Cyril lets out a fake laugh.

"On behalf of Maurice," Paulette declares, "I propose a toast to all his benefactors! To Yolanda! To Yolanda! To François, a hero!"

The physical therapist holds out his hands, conveying that he was simply doing his job.

"To François! To Margarida and João!"

João Fonseca stands up and says, tearfully, "To Monsieur Sokolov, our darling of the building!"

"To Tamara," Paulette continues, "his oldest girlfriend! To Tamara!"

"I don't see why that's worth toasting to," Tamara says.

"Oh, don't be so modest!"

"First off, I wouldn't say oldest, but longest-lasting. The longest-lasting of his girlfriends."

"The longest-lasting of his girlfriends! And the most exasperating!"

"She just can't keep quiet," Tamara whispers to me. "She's a chatterbox who's got to fill every single moment."

"Don't mind me, I'm deaf," Paulette says.

"Deaf but not mute," Tamara shoots back.

"But where's Albert?" I ask.

Tamara stares at me, alarmed. Maddie leans over and whispers, "We buried him a month ago."

"What about Auschwitz?" Paulette shouts; she might have gotten started on her beloved champagne a bit too soon. "You haven't told us about Auschwitz! They went to Auschwitz with their sister. How was it, my darlings? It was horrifying, wasn't it?"

"Oh, so you've been!" Cyril says. "It's a must, isn't it? I'll tell you, I came back transformed." (The Clinton chin again.)

"Transformed . . . into what?" Serge asks.

The Fonsecas can barely keep up.

Tamara shakes her head in a constant bewildering motion.

Serge gets up. "If you'll excuse me, I'll have a smoke by the window."

"Oh, I'll come with you!" Maddie says, suddenly excited. "If you don't mind terribly."

"Being all polite now, are we?"

"Well, forgive me for having some manners! I'm in a state, you know."

Tamara says, "That girl will play the coquette all the way to the grave, honestly."

"Spit your venom, Tamara!"

I smile at the nurse. She's a beauty, sitting prim and quiet.

Paulette sprawls out on the couch. "Remember, Cyril, when Maurice pulled out of the Cronstadts' and rear-ended the car and flattened their whole bed of hortensias? Ha ha ha! It was pitch-black out and he couldn't see the speedometer. Oh, that was hilarious!"

Cyril smiles like an American with teeth that strike me as oddly larger than last time.

"What's become of the Cronstadts?"

"They're all dead, my darling! Everyone's dropping like flies these days, you know. François, I made these salmon canapés just for you."

"I've had three already," says the physical therapist.

Paulette gets up and flips on a light switch.

"No! Turn off that ceiling light, Paulette, for God's sake," I burst out.

As we head out, I take her aside. "Nobody told me Albert Blum died," I say.

"Well, naturally . . . Tamara put him in a home, he lasted all of three days."

I ask her to explain Maurice's change of heart. After nagging and nagging at me to help him end it, he'd stopped talking about it. Even before his heart attack, he seemed to have accepted his fate.

"Antidepressants," she whispers in my ear.

"Did he know?"

She shakes her head. "Can you imagine! I crushed the pill and stirred it in his yogurt."

∽

In the cab back, I ask Serge: "On a desert island: Ramos Ochoa or Cyril Sokolov?"

"Too hard."

"Especially since neither of them can hunt or chop down a tree."

He nods. He thinks. And then, finally:

"Cyril Sokolov."

I have to agree. He's had a life. He can talk about Massachusetts.

∽

Paulette's answer has set off an obsessive earthquake inside me.

I tell myself, eyes wide open in the dark, that I'd been ready to mix the lethal drink with my own hands, yes, really.

The humiliating orders not to get involved aside, I actually was inclined to hand him the glass with a straw. I'd suffered through the outraged, belittling tirade of Professor

Soulié-Ortiz, who, I'd been informed, could—under the right circumstances—deliver the magic potion.

You didn't back down; the second I came through your bedroom door, you said, "How are things looking?" I admired your toughness in wanting yourself gone, Maurice, I admired it as much as the panache that's colored your whole life. I was your brother in arms. You chose me and I was the man for the job. I'll get the recipe, I'd promised myself, I'll do what it takes to get you out of this gloomy mess your life's become. One teensy pill crushed up in some yogurt and buh-bye to the whole daredevil thing, I think, lying down, bitter and stiff. The walks with the physical therapist and that whole jumble of tubes (after you'd been deemed a lost cause on all fronts), the salmon you were eating again, the beloved champagne in the evenings was just to keep the peace, that's what I told myself, so the whole swarm of folks pampering you and scolding you wouldn't be disappointed, yes, I was telling myself that, and I really did think, at my best moments, as harrowing and wonderful as you are, the most impatient man in the world, you resigned yourself to the matter. You made your peace with it all, and I have to say, I was actually disappointed. When you stopped being so determined, I think as I stare at the ceiling, I rued how you'd been so unfaithful to yourself, and more broadly, the tendency beings have to adapt to absolutely anything, to resign themselves to the most degrading of hells. At the same time, I thought, bound up at your bedside in conflicting worries, how can I not pull back to the edge of that massive, gaping hole? Animals freeze when they smell death. If only you'd bucked up! If only I'd seen a glimmer of fear or revulsion! No, you just looked resigned, you went calmly to the slaughter. We need some sort of model to validate our conception of man. You were my model, Cousin Maurice. You flinched and all you did was betray me. And now this pill crushed in your yogurt! That's the worst part of it: the yogurt, I think, how did you land on yogurt? No doubt spoon-fed by one of your nurses. Vanilla yogurt and a powder against dark thoughts to kick your synapses into gear, I think as I turn on the bedside lamp, as if in your doldrums and your frailty death were a dark thought. You were betrayed, my poor Maurice. Paulette and the doctor oversaw your end, naturally. And you had no idea. But you accepted the yogurt. "His yogurt," Paulette was so fond of saying. A dessert fit for the young and the old. Did the yogurt, this inherently criminal non-food, come into play because of some hidden inclination or because of the influx of serotonin in your nervous system? If it's the latter, I think as I get up to pour myself a glass of vodka, what exactly did those bitches crush the very first pills into?

∽

Marion's explained that the fatty mass rounding out the top of women's backs and catapulting them into another era is called a buffalo hump. That buffalo hump set in sharp relief by her hair pulled into a ponytail is what I see that sleepless night, her head forward and her phone against her ear. The red bag strap across her chest and belly. Her unsure steps on the gravel. The two train cars that I'm still not sure are originals or reconstructions, if it even matters, I feel like it does although I don't know why. It's my sister's body that I see, and our solitude along the railroad tracks. I don't think of the thousands of deportees absurdly transported there in another century but of my sister's aged body. Maybe it's not so much her aged body as her energy poured into a void, her head bowed, her legs heavy and driven by unreadable hopes. Or rather her thick dark blue jeans in a hybrid cut chosen for purportedly relaxed comfort and character but just underscoring her age and the guillotine between past and present. I feel pity for those useless train cars. I feel pity for the woman full of goodwill who came so far with her red bag. Tonight, I can clearly see our weightlessness, our nothingness.

∽

Serge tells me in an overexcited voice on the phone that he's got two bits of good news. I immediately think, aware all the while of how unreasonable such a thought has to be: no more heart trouble, no more blotches on lungs. To be honest, the blotch worries me more than the heart. In any case, it's not this, that, or the other thing. He's found an apartment for Joséphine. The apartment is a third-floor thirty-five-square-meter one-bedroom that doesn't have another building facing its windows in a street above Saint-Lazare. Some cousin of

Patrick Seligmann's (him again!) is currently living there. A sweetheart deal, in Serge's words, thirty percent below market rate. He's only seen photos so far and wants me to go with him. I ask a few questions. Why would this cousin sell it below market rate? "She's in a rush, she's bought a place in Le Midi near her daughter, she doesn't want to get all sorts of agents involved." How's he planning to pay for it? "That's the other bit of good news," he says. "I'll tell you in person."

We head up rue Adalbero-Klein. No shops. A somewhat dull street that doesn't feel in line with Joséphine's temperament. I mention it to Serge. "Did anyone offer you an apartment when you were twenty-five?" he says. "Beggars can't be choosers!" He's in a white shirt, looking thin, I find him in especially good shape. The other good bit of news is that the car lot's been sold to Jean-Guy Aboav, the brother of Jacky Alcan's wife. He tells me how he buttered him up. "So I'm telling him, 'Jean-Guy, first of all, you have to know it's not the real-estate transaction I'm interested in, it's the commercial exploitation of the premises. It's a car lot. I've always liked cars. I wanted to get a retro thing going, what with vintage making a comeback. But now there are online marketplaces where you can get anything and everything you want. You can check out the car with 360° videos that are just like being right there in person and you can do that in bed. The other thing, I've been saying, I'm not interested in doing any of the usual auto shop stuff, repairs and all that. With Norauto and Feu Vert and all those other chains where you can get a service package for 69 euros, what's the point? But you, Jean-Guy, you've got a golden touch. There's nothing but town houses all around. They'll green-light three-story buildings. The sous-prefet will get on it lickety-split. As for city hall, they'll be doing cartwheels and jumping at the excuse to kick-start an urban requalification operation, taking back the road, the storefronts along the street, building by building—the whole neighborhood's going to take off. You'll make a beautiful three-story miracle. You'll be king of the hill!' And I could tell I already had Jean-Guy hook, line, and sinker. 'Let me tell you, Jean-Guy,' I said, 'if I wasn't in such a hurry, nothing in the world would keep me from doing it myself. But the thing is, I have to scare up a nice chunk of change to get Jo a place.' That was the masterstroke. Telling a fellow Jew that you've got to give your daughter a home, that's a nice touch. I capped it off by palming him off to my lawyer, who told him the same things, namely, nothing."

Upon reaching the building, Serge brags about the façade's understated elegance. We walk up. The stairwell smells like grilled meat. A very tiny elevator has been shoved in. The lady who lets us in is minuscule and bouncy. She's got on a tracksuit jacket and a long skirt that's unusually heavy. Serge clutches both her hands in his. She comes up to his chest. She's all smiles. The apartment door leads directly to the main room. When she pulls back to let us take in the space, she does so with a hop. The piece is dotted with glass trinkets. They're everywhere. On the coffee table, the dining table, the shelves, the radiator board. There are some tumblers, some balls, some miniature pitchers, hourglasses, or other stills, but the collection is primarily made up of animals, birds, horses, octopuses, cats, bears, roosters in every shade . . . She points out her *wapiti* figurine atop a pedestal which she's apparently very proud of. I compliment it. She laughs and strokes its horns. Serge's already in the bedroom. He calls me so I can see the unobstructed, melancholy view. A low wall, above which protrudes the roof of an abandoned workshop, some ivy, a few gnarled trees. "Charming, isn't it?" he remarks, a hint of awe in his voice. At that very moment, the ground starts shaking, a terrifying roar comes from the walls, the whole menagerie crashes together in a concert of high-pitched clinking chimes. It takes a few long seconds for everything to settle again. Our hostess folds a napkin and puts it away under the coffee table. She doesn't seem to have noticed the phenomenon.

"What was that, Madame Ehrenthal?" Serge says.

The little lady chuckles. "Oh, the métro! It does that every two minutes. My darlings just have a blast!"

Outside, we cross the street to see the nice workshop up close. From the apartment window, I'd noticed a sign on the low wall. Pinned to the construction permit is an overview image showing a fifteen-story building complex. I point it out to Serge with a stern finger.

∽

Marion's found a way to dress Luc up to the point I can barely recognize him. She's put him in a sleeveless waistcoat over a little Catholic's blue-polka-dot shirt, overly ironed gray pants, and shoes that might as well be wooden clogs. I'm not going to talk about the hairstyles straight out of those class photos from the sixties. He looks like a village idiot dressed up as a pageboy.

"It's a kids' birthday party!" I tell Marion.

She thinks he's handsome. She agrees to get rid of the waistcoat. She's not backing down on the rest.

The car is parked on a side street. Marion waves goodbye through the window. I wait until we're far away to rumple his shirt and tousle his hair a bit. Luc doesn't put up a fight; he's stock-still. In the car, I tell him where we're going. I talk to him about Marzio, Valentina, my brother Serge who we're going to pick up. I see him in the rearview mirror only half-listening.

He says, "Your brother?"

"Yes."

"How old is he?"

"My age, a bit older."

I ask if it's all right for me to put on some music. He says yes. I put on Christophe's "Les Mots bleus," the Bashung version.

He sways, smiling. He repeats, "*Je lui dirai, je lui dirai*" . . . It looks like things are good.

Serge is waiting for us outside his place. Summer outfit. Clean-shaven. On the sidewalk is the massive, shoddily wrapped toy crane. He sets it frenetically on the back seat beside Luc.

"We're going to be late! What took you so long?" he asks.

"I had to drive from Bègues."

"Did you bring a present?"

"That book about the universe. All about how matter is made on Earth and in the stars and the galaxies. Nice idea, yeah?"

"Sure. I've got some jitters. I can smoke in the car, right?" He turns to Luc. "Say, kid, any trouble for you if I smoke?" Luc shakes his head no. "You're a good one."

He smokes.

"Don't be so nervous. It'll all be fine."

"Easy enough for you to say."

"She's the one who suggested you come."

"I took two Xénos."

"Serge, we're going to a kids' party!"

"Exactly."

∾

Valentina welcomes us in. Smiling and sweet.

"Marzio! Serge's here!"

Marzio bursts out and hugs Serge. Serge's all tangled up with his present. With his free hand he grabs the base of the boy's face. "Let me see that mug of yours. Does my big guy want to see what I brought him?"

Valentina cheek-kisses Luc. She takes the book about the universe, which I'd handed to him, off his hands. "What's your name?"

"Luc."

"And I'm Valentina."

Valentina says she's happy to see me. Children of various ages are shrieking and running all around. In the sitting room I see a few grown-ups, mainly women.

Marzio's holding the huge package tightly.

"Open it," Serge says.

"What is it?" Valentina asks.

"Not here, not in the front hall!"

But Marzio's already torn the thin wrapping paper off. Out comes the image of the yellow plastic toy against the skyscraper background. "Electric construction crane!" Serge announces.

"In the bedroom," Valentina orders before heading into the kitchen, where she's been summoned. Marzio unexcitedly lugs the box into his bedroom. We follow him. The little room is already overflowing. I notice the packaging for a programmable robot, a waterproof digital photo/camera for kids, various books, an explorer's kit with headlamp, binoculars, compass. On the floor, very little kids are watching a cartoon on an iPad. Marzio opens the box. The crane has to be assembled. The components scatter across the floor. The user's guide is as big as an unfolded Michelin map. Deafening music comes from the living room.

"Arista!" Marzio shrieks as he clambers over us. (Later on, I will learn that this is a singer named Harry Styles.)

Luc kneels and picks up the crane's offset arm.

I say, "Want us to put it together?"

"Yes, let's do it," Serge says.

Luc's already opening all the plastic baggies with the pieces. A little rug rat crawls over to us and takes the bucket. Serge pries it out of his hands. The baby's about to cry and then changes his mind. Serge sits on the bed. The base, the mast, and the boom are easy to assemble; the counterweights, the connections, and the cables aren't any problem. From his perch, Serge smokes and threatens the kid with a nasty look at the least attempt to get close. The pulleys' washers are tiny, I can't see where they should be threaded. Serge gets antsy. Luc wants to do it for me. They're getting on my nerves. By the time I've managed to get the traction wires and the hook in place, I'm all wound up.

It's all set. Luc wants to turn on the remote control.

"No, no, me first. I have to make sure it's all good."

The boom goes back and forth. The bucket moves up and down.

"It's working! Marzio! Marzio!" Serge yells from the bedroom door.

"How do you expect him to hear you over this racket?"

He disappears.

I'm thirsty. Even with my joints practically fused together, I manage to stand up. I leave Luc with the crane. In the living room the children are dancing and getting into a mess. Marzio's put on rose-colored glasses and is striking crazy poses with his head that the other children mimic.

What a show-off, I think. It was so stupid to dream we could put these boys together when they were polar opposites.

I bring Luc back a Coke. The babies have abandoned the cartoon to watch him maneuver the engine.

"Don't you want to go dance with the other kids?"

"No."

I go over to Serge, who's bumbling around by the bookcase. "No hint of my books now," he says, "None. She got rid of them all." A woman dances with a toddler and watches us. She moves his arms for him as if that could be charming. It's very hot despite the open window. Not to mention the astounding sound levels due to the music and all the shrieking.

We head into the kitchen in search of cold water. Valentina's almost done putting the candles on the cake. Serge offers to use his lighter for them. He does so deftly.

"*Magnifico!*" Valentina exclaims. She grabs the tray and thrusts it into his hands. "Hold this. You carry it! And, Jean, can you stop the music?"

Valentina leads a small procession while intoning the Happy Birthday song. Serge follows with the cake. He's singing, too, immersed in his unexpected role. I go get Luc. In the narrow hallways I crash into a woman repatriating the little ones. Everyone's clustered around Marzio, who's taking his third big breath. "Take off your glasses!" Valentina says. Fourth inhale and puff. All ten candles blown out. Applause. Serge helps serve the slices, passes around the plates. There's also vanilla ice cream. He jokes with the kids, adds a bit of marzipan or a candied leaf for the ones with even more of a sweet tooth. He even places a paper bib around a girl's neck. I've never seen him so eager. Not in my life. Luc ducks into the bedroom as soon as he's been served. The woman who was dancing talks to me. I think she's commenting on the cake. A strawberry plant. Maybe she's asking me who I am. Who I am? Her son tugs on her dress with sticky fingers. She gently pushes him away. She's excruciatingly cheerful. I seem to have a knack for attracting excruciatingly cheerful women. It looks like Serge and Valentina are having a bit of a conversation. An over-the-table conversation, amid other people, sweet nothings flitting around like feathers. She laughs. He can still make her laugh, I realize—it's not all a lost cause. And I feel an inexplicable twinge. Marzio comes back to cling to him, wearing those glasses with pink frames and lenses.

"What are these glasses?" Serge asks.

"Dough Trash's glasses," Marzio says.

"He's going to ruin his eyes," Valentina says.

"The boy hasn't seen his crane yet. Jean put it together."

"Go and look at the crane that Jean put together for you, Marzio!"

"Okay."

Marzio and Serge head into the bedroom. I follow them.

Suddenly I notice the odd noise. The engine skidding that looks just like batteries burning. The threads holding up the bucket have gotten tangled. Luc's trying to untangle them with one hand and fix the setup with the other. The whole mechanism is jammed.

"Stop, stop!" I say.

"What's going on?" Serge asks.

"The wires slipped out of the pulleys and got tangled."

"What did he do! What did you do?"

Luc steps back, terrified.

"He didn't do a thing. This toy's very fragile!"

"It's not fragile, it just has to be handled carefully!"

I crouch down as best as I can, my back practically broken.

"We need a letter opener," I say. "Or a pin. The problem is the size of the washers . . ."

"What did he do? It's all messed up! This moron messed it all up!"

He turns to Marzio. "You didn't even see it work! Did you see it shine? It was working perfectly!"

Luc starts crying. Marzio runs off. He shouts, "Ma! Ma!"

I stroke Luc's hair. "It's not your fault, it's this damned thing. Don't cry."

Valentina hurtles in, Marzio two steps behind.

"That thing is ghastly! He can't have it in his room!"

"Why not? It's magnificent!" Serge says.

"There's no space! You can't get around it. You know this room is small! You know it. You *lived* here!"

"Just put it up against the radiator! He's ten. When I was his age, I was happy as a clam in a pigsty!"

"We can't keep this crane. And stop making things about yourself!"

"He wrecked it, anyway."

I push away the boom and set the mast on the ground. "There! Now your crappy crane is properly wrecked."

I get up. "I'm sorry," I tell Marzio.

"I didn't really like it," Marzio says, still hiding in his mother's skirt.

"You know he doesn't care about those sorts of things," Valentina tells Serge.

"No, I didn't know that. What does he care about? PlayStation? His pink glasses? What do you care about, big guy?"

"Come with me, Luc," I say. "Pardon us, Valentina, we'll be going now. Thank you for having us."

"I don't want the boy crying," Valentina says.

"He'll get over it."

I grab Luc's hand and we get out of there.

∽

It's Father I think about when I see Luc's scarlet-red face in the rearview mirror. I think about Father, about his knack for humiliation, about his weakness. A weakness passed down from father to son, inevitably passed down from father to son, no matter how careful or resistant they are: bad faith, limps, bouts of mild insanity; an insidious, oppressive deterioration. I can't go back to Bègues with this dressed-up boy puffy as he holds back tears. What do tears lead to? I think. You weren't any different, Serge, you had a ruddy face, you bit back your tears, you were a sad sack, and now, fifty years later, a vicious moron.

"What do you want to do, Luc? Let's go have a good time somewhere."

I can see his lips move. He's mumbling something.

"Louder, I can't hear you."

"To the swimming pool . . ."

"The swimming pool might be tricky. It's late, we don't have our swimsuits, we don't have anything . . . Tell me the parts of the breaststroke."

"Prayer . . ."

"Praying . . . And then? What's after hands together? Sub . . ."

"Submarine . . ."

"Wait, I have a great idea! You'll like it."

"What is it?"

"It's a surprise."

In the rearview mirror, he looks somewhat happy. The sun's coming through the car window. All is well. Or terrible. Hard to tell.

∽

At the entrance to Les Invalides, I say, "Look, they've brought in a Panzer IV." When I was little, I knew every single German model from WWII. Luc doesn't care at all—he doesn't even know that I'm talking about a tank.

The cannons in the main courtyard intimidate him. "All the big French generals have been buried in this chapel," I tell him. When I was his age, a line like that would have had me seeing all sorts of surreal, macabre visions.

At the museum of relief maps, Luc slowly makes his way around the huge scale model of Bayonne. He pauses momentarily to look at the bridge and the fortress and then goes on down the fields.

"Do you know the name of the river?" I ask. "It's the Adour." I hold back from deluging him with details.

He goes back around the other way, eyes already turned to the scale model of Blaye. He goes to Blaye. He goes from one fort to the next at a snail's pace. He goes around the Château d'If, the Château de Belle-Île, the Château de Perpignan. He wanders from one vitrine to the next. Every so often, he stops to look at the city walls, the fortifications, the sea, the heaps of houses.

I say, "They're like your towns! Look: it's Saint-Tropez!" (But why would he care about Saint-Tropez?) "Look at the Château d'Oléron! Did you see those tiny cones on the salt flats? Aren't these models just beautiful?"

I wish he were running like he still does sometimes. When he's running, then I know he's happy. He's not running. He goes and sits on the floor, in a darkened corner by the pedestal of Vauban's bust.

I grab his hand: "Come with me, I'm going to show you something." I lead him to a room I know about. In there, we look at the tools and materials used to make the scale models. I point out the screw used to drill holes in trees, the sands of various colors and textures in wooden compartments for the roads and paths. The wheel that furrows the fields! All the bristles, all the tinting powders for the reliefs and the crops. Luc presses his face to the glass; he's interested in the tools of the trade.

I take him to the gallery. "Let's see Mont-Saint-Michel. The model was made for Louis XIV by the abbey's monks. Do you know who Louis XIV is?" He does. "You might as well say that it was made for one monk alone!" At Mont-Saint-Michel, Luc comes alive. He circles the island, and again, he ends up running along the sea and the ramparts, he's bouncing, swaying back and forth. I can see him, deep down, in the dark of night, making his way up the steep steps separating the cliffs; with his head down I can still tell that he's taking a rampart walk.

I ask, "Where would you live?"

Once he's finished exploring the towns, he asks me where I would live. He goes back around, staring. He'd live at the top of the fortification in front of a semicircular tower.

"Yes, yes, not a bad idea!"

"What about you?"

I pause. I'd noticed a house in the village with a little yard but I'm worried it doesn't have a view. I say, "Come and look, Luc. The monks' cells." I light them up with my phone's flash. Bed, table, religious images. He glances quickly at the hidden parts of the monastery, the paintings inside the church that can't be seen without this light, and he's gone somewhere in the stone streets. He's Luc again. All is well. Or terrible. Hard to tell.

∽

Traffic jams on the way out of Paris. I call Marion as I drive. She's on the verge of tears after yet another argument with the downstairs neighbor. Today it's about watering. The water from Marion's plants is dripping onto the neighbor's tray of geraniums and leaving muddy splotches on his windows. "Like I'm doing it on purpose!" she says. "As it is, I barely dare to water the poor things. My bellflowers are practically wilted! Was your thing fun?"

"Sure."

"He said I need a proper fuck."

"Oh, so he's met the Argentine guy."

"That's not funny! He's a sicko. I want you to come over and chew him out."

"We're stuck in traffic."

As I hang up, I tell Luc, "We're going to say that the birthday party was boring. There's no point telling her about the crane and my stupid brother. I'm ashamed of him, you know."

Luc's quiet.

"And Marzio! I was so excited to introduce you! I've never seen such a stupid kid."

Marion opens the door in a bathrobe and her hair in an African turban. She's still wet from her shower and seems less wound up than on the phone. She immediately wants to know all the latest gossip, especially how things look between Serge and Valentina.

I said, "Valentina deserves far better."

"What's that got to do with anything?"

"The party was too crowded, too loud. We didn't stay long. I took Luc to see the scale-model fortified villages at Les Invalides."

"Did he get along with Valentina's boy?"

"Quite well."

She plops down onto the corner couch and pulls Luc in close.

"Did you get along with the boy?"

He slides onto her lap and curls up in the fetal position. She strokes his forehead.

"We can invite him over one Sunday. I did a natural dye job on my hair. It's making my scalp itch so much. Jean, be a darling, go ring at that imbecile's door and tell him that you'll punch his teeth in if I hear another insult out of his mouth."

"I already go every month."

"Only once. With that gentle, cowardly tone of voice."

"Twice. And you called him brainless."

"Damn right I did! Now, how about if you pour us some vodka?"

I end up beside them with the glasses.

"In Poland, I discovered ginger vodka."

She says, "I need to put him in bed soon. He's got school in the morning."

The TV's on with the sound muted. Shipyard and huge ocean liner. President laughing with his odd upturned nostrils. Ineffable seriousness of participants on a set. Luc's legs stretch out across mine. The room's a welcome mess. A heap of feminine accessories, domestic trinkets, toy components, a whole array of stray objects. Outside, dimming light across the Bègues rooftops. We can hear car doors slamming. The noises of Bègues are unlike those of Paris. These are slightly sad sounds, coming from nowhere. Bègues has no outlying areas. No true limits. Where Bègues ends, another town begins, and where that one ends another one begins, one that's for all intents and purposes the same. In the museum, the towns were distinct within the countryside, human masonry huddled up, settled deep within mystery. Marion's happy living in Bègues. Meaning there is indeed a place called Bègues. If I think of Bègues as a place, I mean a place where I can permanently be, an exile's pain suddenly comes over me. At the museum of relief maps, I could imagine myself in a hovel in Bayonne with war and the unknown all around. Bittersweet is all return. Marion coos things in her son's ear. She's talking to him in a language that doesn't exist. A made-up song from his infancy that she's remembered for him alone. I pour us some more vodka. The TV goes on spitting out its jerky images.

Marion's unwrapped her African turban. She says, "Do you think we're headed into a horrible world?" Then she says, "This boy needs dinner, you've got school in the morning, my love." She twists her hair in her fingers and asks me what color it is now. I act clueless. She laughs. One of Luc's socks has a hole in it. I slip my finger through to tickle him.

∽

I read somewhere that as men get older, they can go two ways. Some put up armor around themselves and get more rigid, others open up and get melodramatic. Uncle Jean is getting melodramatic. At this moment I can be found on one of those modern pavilions adjoining the Bois de Vincennes dancing with my sister to "Jailhouse Rock." An hour ago, in the conference room nearby, with parents on the right and students on the left, we were watching the slow-moving conferral of diplomas from the École Émile Poillot. The DJ set up for the multigenerational group's switching from rap to oldies. A jeering assembly of educated souls—Margot, Joséphine, Victor, other friends from his year—scold us as they sip punch. Jo seems to have recovered from the Tunisian guy's disappearance. Ramos hangs around, never straying far from the buffet and always nibbling with feigned nonchalance. Uncle Jean's taken off his jacket. He twirls his sister around with the fury of an old man. It's a particular fury, dogged and unyielding, a daredevil fury that the man casts off, panting and parched, as he half-heartedly leaves the dance floor, dreaming of being back soon, driven by some deep-rooted mechanism. Uncle Jean sidles up to Ramos, claps his hand on the other man's shoulder, and asks him how the sangria is, after all, he's a Spaniard. Ramos thinks it's decent enough (even if there's too much cinnamon) and rushes over to pour him some (he tosses back a ladleful in doing so) and brags to Jean about the teensy squid fritters and the pepper tapas cooked up by the first-years. The first-years actually did the whole banquet, he says, his face red as a brick from the heat or from the wine. Margot wants to dance with Uncle Jean too. She tugs at his sleeve but the music's changed. She says it's a shame that Uncle Serge isn't here.

"Was he even invited?"

Ramos picks out a tortilla slice and says, "I don't think anyone invited him."

She says, "That's stupid. You're all stupid. Stop stuffing your face, Papa, you're already massive."

On the packed patio I can see Victor curled up with a girl. Unlike his father, he's tall and handsome. I ask Margot if that's his girlfriend. She doesn't know.

She says, "What about you, how come we never see your girlfriend?"

"I don't have a girlfriend."

"Oh, Uncle Jean, I'm sure you're not on your own."

"Don't be such a pest," Ramos says, swallowing a croqueta. I think about the phrase *on your own*.

Nana's joined us; she's dangling off my arm. She says, "It's a nice party, isn't it?"

I kiss her overheated neck and I think: *My dear sister*. A melodramatic man could feel right at home during an Ochoa party. Clapping at the director's speech, tearing up as Victor crosses the stage with his envelope. He thinks that he isn't on his own. He's going to party after party. Yesterday he was at the one for Luc's school. The child made only a brief appearance as a Neapolitan mafioso with sunglasses practically covering his face. Then they went and got pizza. *I'm not on my own*, he thinks. He looks at the large room, the square in front, where families and friends are drinking and eating and celebrating. He's part of this brotherly group; he raises his glass, he laughs, he shoos away the fleeting dark clouds that brush up, shuts his eyes when the abyss opens up that all these carefree people—brothers, sisters, cousins, fiancés and fiancées, the old, the graduates—will fall into.

∽

It's two in the morning. The street's deserted. I immediately make out his dark silhouette, darker than the night. Perched atop one of the front doors' guard stones, the crow of rue Grèze awaits me. I say *the* crow because this is clearly the crow that was pecking apart the dead pigeon a few months ago.

What's it doing here at this hour? It saw me from afar and watches, unmoving and impertinent like Poe's raven: *Perched upon a bust of Pallas just above my chamber door— / Perched, and sat, and nothing more*.

I ask, out loud, "What do you want?"

It stares at me, unblinking.

"What's your name?" I ask. "Tell me your name."

I listen carefully, waiting for its utterance *Nevermore!* in its native tongue, like its fictional predecessor. But it is silent. A statue upon its plot of stone.

In a Spanish village where I was walking one long-distant night with a girl I liked, we were trailed by a procession of black birds. Come from nowhere and dogging our steps in a long, unnerving, sluggish train. It was hot out. I held Ariane by the waist and we made our way in silence between the unlit houses trying to find a direction in the living chaos. She was the sort of girl from my childhood who lingered from one corner of the world to the other. Her hair smelled like incense, she had amulets and powder in her pockets. What became of those people who pulled away?

The crow flaps its wings and then tucks them again. In other periods of my life, I wouldn't have thought twice about this presence, I wouldn't have remained at the doorstep obsessed by the icy darkness of its plumage and its funereal beak.

What fragility (cowardice) paralyzes me before this fowl? Fly off, you scavenger. Off you go. Let me go back inside, you sinister beast.

∾

As summer returns, so does time. Nature laughs in your face. The spirit of bliss skins your soul. One summer holds all the summers, the summers past and the summers we will never see. Last summer our mother was still alive. She was slowly declining in her ground-floor Asnières place under the watchful eye of more or less compassionate caretakers, fighting from bed to kitchen chair where she sat to eat nothing against unceasing nausea. For almost two weeks we'd left her alone with those security guards. We hadn't seen the point of scheduling our trips in shifts so she wouldn't be abandoned. I'd call her from Vallorcine, where I was on mountain expeditions. She'd speak in a reedy voice that tortured me and she almost never complained. With each call I'd follow up with Serge (in Greece with Valentina) or Nana (in their Torre dos Moreno shack). They did likewise. Each time we'd wonder if one of us shouldn't head back, but nobody did.

Some summers come from further back. The summer of black birds, on the road to Portugal. The summer of hiking the GR20 in Corsica and the two dogs we'd walked with that had chased our car. The summer of my exams. The summer of Jerusalem on the bus with Serge. Even further back, a summer in Roger Oudot Square, Nanny Miro on a bench, her limp bag set beside her and inside it another soft bag out of which stuck balls of wool and the yarn she was knitting with. A long series of images that, lodged in an ordinary brain, will disappear with it. Images with no significance and no connection other than with the treacherous gleam of summer, this blade that comes back every year to slice us again.

∾

He calls me on July 20. Twenty, a fine number. Two plus zero equals two. A calming, amiable number. He was careful to choose that date for the second scan. He's just come out. It's been a month since we've talked. In the days following Marzio's birthday, I'd hoped for some sign, an indication, no matter how indirect, to preserve his self-respect. But nothing doing. He informs me that the nodule's twice as big.

"Twice?"

"It's gone from six millimeters to eleven."

"What did the technicians tell you?"

"What were you hoping they'd say?"

"Where are you?"

"Walking down the street."

"How are you feeling?"

"I've never felt so good in my life."

Two days later, I take him to the pulmonologist. A tall, spare man who isn't quite old or young, with uneven bangs hanging across his forehead. On the wall, above him, is a poster with a conceptual image of the South Pole. He waves us in with an aghast look that seems to be permanently stuck on his face. He runs through the scan results and confirms, with little emotion, that the nodule's size has likely grown. Then he inserts a CD into the computer and settles into his chair to study the images. A mobile AC blasts chilled air through the room. The quiet clacking of the keyboard cuts through the whirring. Serge has on bulky, cardboard-like blue jeans. I haven't seen him wear jeans in years. And he doesn't know how to wear them. Did he put them on to look young, or to try to look ordinary? The pulmonologist just keeps peering at the screen. Serge watches him, his hands together between his legs, his upper body positioned in concave immobility. I come to realize that he isn't actually looking at the doctor but at the Antarctic's blue amid the gray continents on the poster. He's staring at this friendly blue, this blue that's positive despite being light, light blue being related, he'd once told me, to lace frills, and thereby not as satisfying but still sufficiently active in the absence of dark blue. The window overlooks a courtyard that is being restored. Every so often, shadows flit across the net curtains. The muffled voice that emerges in the silence says, "We'll need to do some further tests."

The pulmonologist suggests a bronchial endoscopy, which involves running a tube through the nose and the throat to biopsy the trachea and bronchi. The pulmonologist doesn't rule out a bacterial infection. "Tuberculosis or another torpid infection could result in this sort of image," he says. The words "bacterial" and "tuberculosis" are immensely comforting; their fictional scale bode well. But he immediately ruins it all with his second prescription: a PET scan. "A PET scan," he says in a horribly gentle voice, "is a more sophisticated procedure that will show us the nature of the nodule and likely detect other anomalies beyond the lungs."

We know what PET scans are, kiddo, I think. We did them at Sarcelles with Mother. Gloomy dawn. Interminable hours in the waiting room. I don't want to hear that music again. Suddenly I flash back on images of years in the mountains with Father and Maurice. Maurice's white loafers, which Father called "rue Raffet slippers," that had him slipping and falling as we extricated him from briar bushes. We gorged ourselves on raspberries and wild strawberries, talking endlessly about their various qualities. Wild raspberry is better, or rather, more predictable, than strawberries on the whole, you can be sure how they'll taste. Between a raspberry and a wild strawberry, side by side, the raspberry is very likely to taste better, but no raspberry can possibly measure up to a perfect wild strawberry. On that point we were always in agreement, I think. While the pulmonologist talks about radiolabeled compounds, tracing agents, public aid, the Centre Cardiologique du Nord, I think about Zita's son slipping down a chasm of waterlilies to pluck a raspberry further down. The waterlilies masked the steepness and he'd fallen into the mountain stream.

"If it takes up glucose, then what?" Serge asks.

"Then that'll be an argument for something active and malignant," the man says with his aghast face.

"A cancer," Serge says.

"That's one hypothesis."

"What do we do after that?"

"It's possible that it may need to be removed. But it isn't reasonable to consider that before getting all the details. I can't present you with all the hypothetical diagnoses and treatments at this stage."

∽

On the sidewalk are two wood pigeons in an incomprehensible mating ritual. The male seems to be utterly obsessed. He follows her, his beak in her feathers, mimicking every step of her erratic trajectory. They suddenly separate and go in opposite directions. She gently returns to him. He doesn't care, goes on pecking at something by the tree's grille and fluttering around to land a meter off. She turns around. He comes back and spins around, puffing himself up.

The waiter brings two coffees and two vodkas.

Serge says, "Not a word to Joséphine."

"No."

"Tuberculosis! Since when has tuberculosis resulted in a tumor?"

"He mentioned aftereffects. A benign nodular aftereffect."

"Benign. Just to smoke me out."

"Are you on your own tonight? Come have dinner with me. I'll make us pasta with garlic."

He nods. We sit in silence.

It's hot out. The chestnut tree's starting to shed its leaves.

After a minute, Serge says: "Peggy Wigstrom's getting married."

"Really?"

"To an insurance broker."

"You should get rid of that hideous plant."

"You think so?"

"Off with it. I'll help you out."

"Maybe I'll find out I just have an infection."

"Who knows."

"A little infection. So much the better!"

"So much the better."

"Or a full-out cancer."

"Don't overthink it."

We sip at our vodka. I order two more.

"Make it a double," says Serge.

"Why do I have to bother with the endoscopy? Why can't I just go straight for the damn PET scan?"

"Because maybe it's just an infection."

He lights yet another Marlboro Gold. The female pigeon has stretched herself out flat. Her hopeful's mounted her in a flapping of manic wings.

"Well, so much for the best days," he says.

"Yeah, all the best days are behind us. But we haven't had our last laugh yet."

He nods. "You know what I want to see? *Young Frankenstein*."

"Me too," I say.

"Remember how Papa burst out laughing? He was never one to laugh."

"It was so embarrassing."

"Everyone in the theater was looking at us. But we were happy!"

∞

"When you smoke two packs a day," Nana says, "you can't act surprised!"

My informing Nana (by phone) of the nodule in Serge's lung and its growth had set off an irrational, wild upheaval. I'd been careful to present matters in a detached, calm manner, reaffirming the bacterial hypothesis, but after two words she wasn't listening anymore. Serge had made his bed with his life of excess and unathleticism, his rejection of any and all discipline. She'd seen for herself in Poland how he was just a boy with no self-control. What did this continual lack of drive mean if not a self-destructive impulse?

She blamed herself for telling him his life was a failure. By what measures was or wasn't life a failure? She herself had been distraught when considering her own life. She'd bothered to care about others far too late in life and saw her belated swerve toward charity as a jump to regain a path leading somewhere. But she owed these things she could do to her entourage and her emotional stability, two things that Serge couldn't claim for himself. To tell the truth, she'd sensed that he was a little out of sorts at Auschwitz. She was a bit of a shaman (her word) and could sniff out those things. He'd struck her as tired and morose, like he had a gray cloud around his head.

"But, good God, how could we have such a catastrophe come down on us in the space of a second! Are we going to have to go through the exact same thing we did with our parents? Long waiting-room hallways and torment, the small glimmer of hope. And why does this illness have to strike our family?"

I cut her off. I was trying to explain that any diagnosis was premature. I did my best to offset her words with some half-baked serenity, and this role of peacemaker struck me as fake and painfully self-interested. What was she supposed to do? Call him? Would he be nice when he picked up?

She asked me how he'd taken it.

I said, "He's brave." But that word seemed meaningless too.

There was a pause in the conversation and I thought I could hear sobbing. I could feel my eyes welling up, too, and I held my breath so she wouldn't know.

In Jerusalem, I'd followed Serge down the cluttered alleyways of the old Arab Quarter. We'd broken off from the group and I felt intoxicated by freedom in this unknown space. I followed my brother through the crowd. I was scared of losing him. My brother looked back to make sure I was there. I waved my hand to reassure him. I've always followed Serge. He complained about it when we were little. In the rue Pagnol apartment, he moved with a constant hanger-on dogging his steps.

∾

The bronchial endoscopy hadn't produced any new results. No infection, no lucky pneumonia.

To the list of major criminals, I would add certain decorators, I think, as I look at the empty row of chairs on a blue beam parallel to ours, screwed to the facing wall. Apart from these seats, there is nothing whatsoever. A smooth, grayish-brown floor under fluorescent lights. No table, no plants; in the corner of the hallway a water fountain can just barely be made out. At eye level, on the gray walls, is a light-green frieze. "Let's decorate this bunker with a little bit of springtime décor," those assholes must have thought. Any man sitting in a basement waiting room of the nuclear medicine department of the Madeleine-Brès hospital is plunged into an abyss of solitude. Whether the patient soon to put his body in the machine or the companion neutralized by protocols and his own impotence. There are three of us in the bunker. Glued to the wall on the industrial bench are the three Popper children. We'll always, to each other, be the three Popper *children*.

Nana says, "Last time we were together was at Auschwitz. Now it's the PET scan at Madeleine-Brès. We've got to find more fun things to do."

He turns to her (he's sitting in the middle), pulls her close by the ponytail, and kisses her on the neck.

"What's your husband doing on his own in his shack in Torre dos Moreno?"

"He's fishing for mackerel. Margot's going to meet him."

"What about the great chef?"

"He's a *second de cuisine* in a new restaurant by Lafayette. But there's only two of them."

"What about the fast-food concept?"

"In the fall."

She maneuvers to lean against him and pat his back, but the seats aren't made for closeness.

After the endoscopy, we'd chucked Seligmann's plant. The pot, the PVC pipe, the hooks—all in two huge garbage bags. That plant was trash.

A nurse comes in and says, "Monsieur Popper?"

Serge Popper gets up. He's holding his medical records like a good student.

He leaves, between the two of us, a bluish hole.

YASMINA REZA is a novelist and playwright whose prodigious work has been translated into more than thirty-five languages. Her plays include *Conversations after a Burial*, *The Passage of Winter*, *The Unexpected Man*, *Art*, *Life x 3*, *A Spanish Play*, *God of Carnage*, and *Bella Figura*, many of which were multi-award-winning international successes. *Art* was the first non-English-language play to win the American Tony Award. *God of Carnage*, which also won a Tony Award, was adapted for film in 2012 by Roman Polanski. Her novels include *Babylon*, which won the Prix Renaudot and was shortlisted for the Prix Concourt, *Hammerklavier*, *Desolation*, *Adam Haberberg*, *Happy Are the Happy*, and *Anne-Marie the Beauty*. She lives in Paris.

JEFFREY ZUCKERMAN is a translator of French literature. His work centers on contemporary fiction from mainland France and Mauritius—including Ananda Devi, Shenaz Patel, and Carl de Souza—as well as texts of the queer canon, including Jean Genet and Hervé Guibert. A recipient of the PEN/Heim Translation Grant, the French Voices Grand Prize, and a National Endowment for the Arts Translation Fellowship, he has been named a Chevalier de l'Ordre des Arts et des Lettres by the French government.